RETURN TO GEDROSIA

By

Allia Irusak

CONTENTS

Chapter 1	5
Chapter 2	15
Chapter 3	27
Chapter 4	37
Chapter 5	45
Chapter 6	49
Chapter 7	57
Chapter 8	65
Chapter 9	70
Chapter 10	75
Chapter 11	91
Chapter 12	96
Chapter 13	104
Chapter 14	114
Chapter 15	127
Chapter 16	137
Chapter 17	145
Chapter 18	148
Chapter 19	152
Chapter 20	160
Chapter 21	179
Chapter 22	185
Chapter 23	188

Chapter 24	193
Chapter 25	203
Chapter 26	211
Chapter 27	220
Chapter 28	224
Chapter 29	231
Chapter 30	233
Chapter 31	236

PART I

The Journey

CHAPTER 1

The Journal

The Beade Academy in Kolachi was a quaint red-brick building, nestled in one of the oldest districts of the city. Staring out the window of her third-floor dorm room was Jahan "Jay" Jumander. It was a view she'd seen a thousand times, but she gazed out with particular interest this morning. She wanted to commit the scene to memory; this might be the last time she saw it, after all.

It was a bright, sunny day, and a cool sea breeze blew in through the large arched windows of her room. Great white clouds floated gently across a deep blue sky. It was recess, and the dusty courtyard beneath her was filled with students playing a variety of games, their laughter and yells of a light, happy sound. Teachers stood on the periphery in the shade of lush cedar trees, chatting amongst themselves as they sipped their tea. These were kind teachers, and this was a great place for these kids, especially since almost all of them were orphans, like her.

Although, they weren't *exactly* like her. Most of these kids had lost their parents during the disastrous Bot Wars. And she'd lost her parents too…but she wasn't quite sure where and how.

She looked at the old leatherbound journal lying on her bed and sighed. It had been such a promising lead…

There was a knock on the half-open door, and a face popped in. It was Erol, her best friend at the Academy.

"You done packing, Jay? Dr. Salim has been messaging me non-stop, asking me if you're done," he said, now standing in the room with hands on hips like a disappointed uncle. He was a lanky teen with long, pulled-back hair and a youthful, narrow face. The expression on his face was one she was all too familiar with his Seriously-Concerned-Adult expression, one she got to see quite often. Jay grinned.

"Yeah yeah, both of you old men need to calm down. Here, look at this."

She picked up the journal, blew dust off its cover, and began leafing through the pages.

"I found this last night Erol, when I was packing in Uncle Salim's attic. At first, I didn't think much of it, lying forgotten behind random knickknacks, but when I opened it...Erol, this belonged to them!"

Erol was still standing by the door, trying his best not to get pulled into whatever this latest wild goose chase was. And he was sure it was going to be a wild goose chase; Jay's wide eyes carried the tell-tale sparkle, and she had that jittery excitement in her voice. But who was he kidding; he'd never quite learned how to resist getting swept up when she was in this sort of mood, and inevitably ended up tagging along for whatever latest wild adventure she had cooked up. No point wasting time, then. He sighed and walked towards her.

"Your parents, you mean?" he asked.

"Yes! And more than that, I think it contains directions to Gedrosia!"

"Uh-huh," Erol said.

She leafed through the pages, finally landing at a hand-drawn map with random numbers and letters scribbled on the border, and pointed at it triumphantly: "There, look!"

Erol glanced at the rough lines of the unlabelled map which could literally have been showing anything, then looked at her eager, excited face, and gave her a small smile. Unlike Jay, his belief in Gedrosia was speculative at best. Some thought that Gedrosia had been an ancient civilization far greater than any other the world had seen, and others thought it was a fable concocted by the Greek traveller Herodotus. Erol didn't really care either way. All he knew was his best friend had been obsessed with finding the place, ever since she'd learned that her parents had died in their own quest to find it. And despite how unlikely it was that this journal was going to lead anywhere, he wasn't going to shoot her dreams down for no reason.

"Okay, maybe," he said. "How do you know it's your parents', though?"

She sighed impatiently, and flicked to the front of the journal, where two signatures were scrawled on the first page. "I'd recognize those signatures anywhere," she said.

"And Dr. Salim, did you ask him?"

Jay frowned. "Not yet. I doubt he wanted me to find this, since it was hidden away in his attic. He'll probably scold me." She then pulled her mouth down and deepened her voice, giving her impression of her uncle, Salim: "Dear child, you must look to the future, and leave the past behind where it belongs, you must!" It was a pretty good impression, and both of them laughed.

"Mind if I take a look?" Erol asked. Jay handed it over, almost bouncing with excitement. Erol skimmed through the faded pages. It was an odd journal, with lots of hand-drawn maps, as well as what looked like schematics for a city. Other scribbles included dates and numbers, and all of it seemed to be encoded somehow.

"This doesn't make much sense to me, to be honest," he said finally, handing it back to a disappointed Jay. "So, where is Gedrosia?"

Jay shrugged, and stared at the journal some more, hoping it'll suddenly reveal its secrets. "That's what I'm trying to figure out."

Erol nodded. Then, gently: "Come on, let's go to the beach. It's your last day here, you know."

Jay felt a sinking feeling in her stomach at being reminded of that. She was moving to Panjgur with her uncle Salim, who had received a tenured professorship at the University of Panjgur. The plans for the move had been brewing over the past year, and they were to move as soon as Jay completed her freshman year of high school. She had already been enrolled for the Fall in the Musk School in Panjgur - an all-girls elite school which, much to her dismay, was full of girls she had no remote connection to. But she was left with no choice. According to Uncle Salim, her parent's last wishes were for her to get an excellent education, and supposedly, this school was it.

She sighed, snapped the journal shut, and put it in her backpack, pushing the sinking feeling aside. It was her last day, and she wasn't going to waste it moping around. She grinned at her friend.

"Let's go, Erol," she finally said, "I know just what we can do!"

They quickly charged out of the hostels and took an e-bus to their favourite spot in town: the GameRoom, where there were tons of virtual games at their disposal, and even a pool table. They fussed over who was the better player at each game they tried – a pretty typical conversation for them - and then headed out to eat, grabbing two plates of spicy salsa beans from the small roadside restaurant that had been Jay's favourite ever since she was a kid. Hunger satisfied, the two headed to Clifton Beach and walked along the shore.

It was late afternoon, the sun a deep orange orb hanging low in a darkening sky. The light, playful banter between them at the GameRoom had given way to a sober, thoughtful silence.

Jay walked with her feet submerged in the cool water and her head bowed, staring as the waves lapped around her ankles. Her thoughts drifted over snippets of the life she was leaving behind: the familiar routines, places, and people that she had grown so fond of over the years.

And her thoughts kept returning to that journal. It was the key to finding where her parents went; she was sure of it. She just wasn't sure how, and that was unbearably frustrating.

Erol walked beside her, occasionally glancing at his friend. She looked about as pensive as he'd ever seen her. He knew her well enough to know she was probably thinking about that journal. He was almost certain it was a dead-end, but he wasn't going to tell her that. He couldn't imagine what it was like for Jay; not ever knowing if your parents are dead or alive, always holding on to the tiniest hope that they may still be out there. He felt bad for her, and he felt a sadness of his own that she was leaving. She was quite reckless and got him into all sorts of trouble, but she was his best friend, and they'd had some great adventures over the years. Despite the sinking feeling in his chest, he forced a smile on his face, and spoke:

"So, are you going to visit often, or forget about us small timers when you get to that fancy school?"

Jay smiled thinly. "I don't know, Erol," she said. "I'll have classes, so…in the summer, maybe."

"Sure, that's soon enough. We can have some fun. Boro will be back too."

"Oh, that'll be nice. I haven't seen Boro in a while."

Boro, or officially BORO1, was Erol's bot, an older model of bots. Next summer, that idiotic rule banning bots from campuses would finally expire, and they could be reunited. It annoyed Erol that he couldn't come sooner, but people were paranoid about robots ever since the Bot Wars. Oh well.

"Yeah," Erol said, "we can finally go up north, and see if there's any truth to the claims of the lost Kalash treasure, or – Jay, what is it?"

Jay's face has turned sadder than he'd ever seen, and she seemed to be on the brink of crying. "I want to go on an adventure now! One last adventure before I have to go to that lame school! Ugh Erol, I hate having to leave so soon." she said.

Erol sighed. "I know. Sorry."

They walked on a bit longer, and though neither knew it, they were both thinking the same thing: goodbyes suck.

The sun had almost set, and the sky had darkened considerably. Jay absently walked away from the shore, then turned to Erol, her eyes still downcast. She willed herself to look up at her best friend and smiled.

"Bye Erol. I'll be coming next summer. First round at the GameRoom on me. You better practice till then, today was way too easy."

Erol grinned. "Challenge accepted. See you around, Jay."

She walked back towards the city to catch an e-bus to Uncle Salim's house. Erol watched her for a while, then continued walking along the beach, staring out at the tiny lights of the ships far out in the distant waters.

※※※

"Are you all packed?"

A rotund man, with wire-rimmed spectacles, wild, wispy hair, and a thick moustache, Dr. Salim Sarmo managed to look every bit the scatterbrained genius professor that he was. Jay smiled at him as she sealed off another box containing her childhood memorabilia. "Almost."

"I know it's hard," Salim came into her room and leaned against a stack of boxes, wiping his forehead with a handkerchief. "To be leaving everything behind. But you'll settle in in no time."

"I just wish I could have spent the summer here. Just one last summer. This was so sudden. I haven't even had a chance to say goodbye to all my friends." Jay stopped her packing and sat down on her bed, looking dejected.

"We spoke about this, Jay." Salim said firmly. "You and I both know it's best to start our lives in Panjgur before your school year starts. You will have ample time to make friends, and I'll even take you to university so you can start the process sooner."

"You're making it sound like a chore. Making friends."

"Well, it is," Salim pushed his spectacles up his nose and sat down beside her. "Lots of variables you know, lots of factors when one wants to engage with other people."

"Oh, I'll be fine, Uncle Salim. I'm not an introverted academic like you." She took his hands in hers, and they smiled at each other. "There's...something else," she said, as she fumbled in her backpack and took out the journal. "I found this when I was cleaning up in the attic. It was theirs, wasn't it?"

Salim stared at the journal with a strange expression on his face, then slowly took it. It was as though he had seen a ghost. "I...haven't seen this for so many years, Jay." He opened it, and absently stared at the signatures scrawled on the first page.

Jay spoke softly, which was really difficult to do because of the excitement in her chest, "does it...have to do with Gedrosia?"

Salim jerked in surprise, and snapped the journal shut. "Gedrosia, again with that nonsense? Listen Jay, I'm really sorry, but your parents are dead. This journal doesn't mean anything. Your father and mother were fond of keeping several of these, for every imaginable purpose. And the fact that they left it behind at my house means it can't be all that important at all. Please, Jay, you must leave the past where it belongs, and look to the future. You must. It's what they would have wanted."

Jay felt the hope fade. "If you say so, Uncle."

"Now, child," Salim said, gentler this time, "don't be so dejected. It doesn't suit you. And forgive this old man if he doesn't have the right answers to give you comfort. I'm just trying to keep the promise I made to your old man."

Jay smiled at the old professor. He had been thrust into parenthood the way she had been thrust into orphanhood, with no real choice in the matter, and definitely no closure. And he was trying his best.

"Tell you what," Salim said, putting an arm awkwardly around her, "why don't you stop packing for tonight. Take some time to get your bearings. I'll take care of the rest of it tomorrow morning. Deal?"

Jay nodded, hugged him back, and watched him exit the room, mumbling to himself as he shut the door behind him.

She stared at the journal for a bit, then began leafing through the pages, finally ending up on the map with random symbols scrawled around it. Then, there the same symbols popped up on some other pages. Oh, if only they'd left some sort of clue, some way to figure out –

Wait.

What was it Uncle Salim had just said? That she should take some time to … get her bearings.

Jay's eyes widened. Bearings. Of course! Even though it was encrypted, the strange letters and symbols surrounding the map *had* to be coordinates.

Coordinates to Gedrosia!

She excitedly pulled out the computer console from her backpack, cleared some of the clutter off her desk, and got to work. It would take some time, but AI-assisted decryption software could very well be used to decipher codes, provided they weren't too sophisticated.

She began with inserting the symbols in the order they were shown. The first set produced no meaningful result. She leafed through the journal and inputted the symbols she found. She programmed the AI to search for words, and then for coordinated. Time flew by. At one point she thought she heard Uncle Salim yell out to her to come for dinner, but she barely heard him. Slowly, the symbols began to decode into meaningful letters and numbers. She thought she found a complete set of coordinates. Then, in parallel, she ran a search through satellite imagery and topographical maps, looking for matches to the hand-drawn map, but allowing enough of a tolerance to factor in inaccuracies in the drawing. She cross-referenced the image data with the coordinates, trying to find the perfect fit, that one place that would match both the map and the numbers...

And after two hours, she thought she had it.

There was a ninety-two percent match. The symbols translated into letters showing a coordinate system and numbers that represented longitude and latitude coordinates. And together, these coordinates pointed towards a location at the small foothills in the Maka province, foothills which looked an awful lot like the hand-drawn map she held in her quivering hands.

She pushed away from the desk and stood up.

Could she actually have found Gedrosia?

Just then her excitement was dampened by the realization that it wouldn't matter in any case. Come tomorrow, she'd be heading in a different direction, and there wasn't much of a chance Uncle Salim would allow her to drive out to the middle of nowhere on what was inevitably a hunch.

Her cell phone rang. For the rest of her life, Jay would wonder about this phone call, and how it seemed to come at the exact right time, and how it irrevocably changed the trajectory of her life forever. Back then, though, she didn't know what was in store, so she simply answered.

It was Erol. He sounded really excited.

"Jay, listen. I know all of this sucks, and it's all really abrupt, and you shouldn't be leaving so soon, well, you shouldn't really be leaving at all, but if you must, you should at least do so after one last adventure you know, because…"

"Erol, what *is* it?!" Jay almost yelled. She had never heard him this excited.

"Well, I just spoke with Dr. Salim, not barely five minutes back, and he told me how sad you were to be leaving, and I told him about the upcoming Indus Robotics Competition, and how I'd love it if you stayed back to help me with the application, and it would only be for a couple of weeks, and then I'd bring you to Panjgur myself, and…Jay, he said yes!"

"My gosh Erol, are you serious?! I'm staying a couple of weeks more?"

"That's right! This is the part where you tell me how amazing I am."

"Oh, you're beyond amazing!"

"Yes yes, that I know. What I don't know is what we should do for one last grand adventure. Any ideas?"

Jay grinned widely. Waves of excitement rippled through her body. "Erol my friend," she said, "I know exactly what we can do."

14

CHAPTER 2

Beginnings

"Slow it, Jay! You're gonna kill us!"

Beads of sweat trickled down Erol's face as the Tezla bounced from one pothole to another on the crumbling, desolate highway.

"Why can't you just use Autodrive like a normal person?" Erol said.

Jay grinned, knowing quite well how tense her friend got by her driving. "What would be the fun of that?"

Just as she said this she yanked at the steering wheel, performing an overly dramatic double swerve to avoid another large pothole.

Finally, she slowed down and turned to Erol, and his expression made her grin even wider. They had left Kolachi that morning, and each kilometre they travelled seemed to lighten her mood further.

"Relax," she said, giving him a playful nudge. "I'm just getting back at you."

"For *what* exactly?"

"For last year," Jay said, "If you recall, you almost got us killed in the Hunza Highlands running after those silly antiques. And the year before, don't get me started on the Volga trip."

"Alright, alright. Just be careful, is all. The last thing we want is an accident, especially out here. *Why* do I let you talk me into this stuff?!"

Erol had managed to convince Salim to let Jay stay back another two weeks, ostensibly to help draft an application to a science camp. But the real reason was so they could have this one final adventure. Salim had agreed on only one condition: that they stay within a 10 kilometre radius of the Academy - a condition which Jay promptly broke first thing in the morning.

And now they were miles away from the city, driving along a rough, unpaved stretch of highway in the Maka province, heading towards the coastal town of Pasni, with a very happy Jay driving like a blind person.

Jay saw the horror-stricken look on Erol's pale face, and nodded sheepishly. "Alright, alright, don't faint on me here. Uncle Salim won't know a thing. Now tell me: are you ready to find Gedrosia?"

Erol shook his head. He knew they were likely chasing a dead end, but he went along, as usual. It was Jay's last adventure, after all. At least they'd be able to explore the Maka province – the outback of the Unit. To explore this region, Erol had to acquire special permits, upgrade his vehicle, retrofit his bot with multiple sensors and gadgets, not to mention acquire fake licenses. But for Erol, it was all in a day's work.

Jay glanced at the navigational console, then at Erol to see if he was sufficiently relaxed. With a smirk, she yanked at the steering wheel and made a sharp turn off the pothole-ridden highway and onto a small, paved service road.

"Watch out!" Erol shouted, as the jeep soared and skidded, rising up for a moment on two sidewheels before crashing down. From behind them they heard a hollow *thud*.

Jay looked back to check on the third passenger on the trip, Erol's bot, BORO1, who had been unusually quiet this entire time.

The 'thud' was from his hard, angular head hitting the jeep's metal chassis. He didn't seem concerned by the impact, his angular face and ruby-like eyes impassive. He stared at her, cocked his head at an angle, and raised his metal arms in an eerily lifelike 'what gives?' gesture. Jay grinned. Boro was a GEN-1, and though he often assured them that he wasn't sentient, Jay had her doubts, given his weirdly humanlike mannerisms.

It had been hours of them driving under the blazing sun, the ground surrounding them parched and cracked. Finally, the oppressive silence of the desert gave way to the distant din of an approaching town.

The Tezla crested a hill, and Jay gasped at the view. In the distance the vast, deep blue Arabian sea shimmered under the afternoon sun. Closer to them, on the shore, was the charming town of Pasni, a snapshot of the past. No high rises towered in the distance, no holographic displays colouring the town, no traffic jams or beeping horns – only a bright mosaic of low-rise white stucco buildings spotted with bright green date trees. It was a quaint little coastal town, even quainter because of the harsh rocky terrain it was nestled in. Jay and Erol exchanged a glance as the Tezla made its way down the hill towards the town.

Pasni was quiet in the late afternoon, especially compared to Kolachi, and they drove through relatively quiet streets and past quiet markets until the nav alerted them that they'd arrived at the guesthouse. Jay manoeuvred the vehicle through a narrow gap in the boundary hedge and pulled up to the elegant mid-century mansion. The guesthouse used to be a twenty-first century post-colonial house, and though some of the wooden balconies seemed unstable, and, overall, it could have used a fresh coat of paint, it was in pretty good condition for something four hundred years old and was far more charming than today's modern metallic motels.

"We actually survived! It's a miracle!" Erol said as he leaped out of the vehicle and raised his arms to the sky in mock-prayer.

Jay shook her head and grinned as she disembarked. They walked towards the guesthouse. A group of guests sitting in the veranda watched them impassively as they sipped on their tea, but their expressions soured when they saw Boro hop out of the Tezla. Jay offered them a polite smile, and Boro awkwardly tried to make himself small and hide behind her. It seemed anti-bot sentiment was still strong in these parts.

The large wooden door to the guesthouse opened and an elderly woman, who went by Mrs. Rani, greeted them with a warm smile. Mrs. Rani, the owner of the guesthouse, was a prim lady with neatly tied silver hair and a softness in her eyes. She also happened to be one of Erol's many aunties. Jay was always perplexed at how Erol happened to either be related to, or somehow knew, every person in the Indus Unit, if not the entire Silk Road Region. Then again, he did have his way around people.

Mrs. Rani ushered the kids into the charmingly old-fashioned reception room, a cute little space made of polished wood, high ceilings, and antique furniture, and greeted them with moist kisses. Besides her relationship to Erol, there was another reason for her affection towards these kids: her eyes were set on Jay as a potential match for one of her many eligible nephews.

After the bare minimum of small talk, she got down to it: "Jahan my dear, would you like to meet my cousin's nephew twice removed? His name's Ali and he's a cryptobanker. You'll love him!"

"Mrs. Rani, not today, I-" But before she knew it, Mrs. Rani had already scurried off somewhere. Seconds later, she bounced back, hand in hand with a smug-looking and fairly handsome teenager, as far as pubescent teenagers go.

"Jay, I'd like you to meet Ali. I was telling you about him earlier. Ali, this is Jahan Jumander, the girl I was mentioning earlier. She studies at the Beade Academy in Kolachi, and her parents, God bless them, were the top archaeologists in the SRR. They're members Academia de Indus, you know."

Ali flicked his hair as his mouth curved into a smile. "Hi Jay."

Jay stared awkwardly at him, forcing the corner of her mouth into a polite smile. "Uh, hi."

With a cocky smirk, Ali handed her a piece of paper, "VR me anytime. My ID's on it." He winked at her and sauntered off.

"Isn't he just lovely?" Mrs. Rani said as she stared dreamily at the boy, "I know he can come across a bit too forward, but can you blame him with that gorgeous golden tan?"

Jay felt a bit of annoyance, but the earnestness in the sweet old lady's face diffused it. Instead, she sighed. "Oh, uh, he's nice, Aunty." She tried her best not to glance behind Mrs. Rani, where Erol and Boro stared at her dreamily, their arms looping high over their heads and meeting at the centre, making a heart shape. "I really appreciate you looking out for me," she said.

"Oh, it's nothing. Girl of your pedigree should have no need to thank me."

Jay pursed her lips, wincing at the word 'pedigree' – a term she felt was more appropriate for a pet than a human. It was this pedigree of hers that, much to her chagrin, had every aunty in the Indus Unit snooping around in her business, trying to play cupid. Little did they know that Jay, unlike most girls her age, had no interest or time for silly notions such as dating and marriage.

"And I'm sure Dr. Salim would approve of the two of you. Speaking of, where is he? I can't imagine he would let you drive here on your own." Mrs. Rani's eyes narrowed.

"Uncle Salim?" Jay gulped and glanced at Erol, who walked towards them, maintaining a calm expression despite the slight nervousness he felt.

"Oh, he did come with us, Aunty," Erol said. "But he had a conference at the, uh, Pasni Science Centre."

"Business in Pasni?" Mrs. Rani seemed surprised. "My, my. I wonder what obscure conference that is. Anyways, all that science stuff is way over my head. I don't suppose he'd be free tonight for dinner?"

Erol shrugged. "Doubt it, Aunty. He said he'd be busy running experiments tonight and wanted absolutely no disturbance. That's why he told us to come here for the night. We'll be picking him up tomorrow morning, and then driving to Panjgur."

Mrs. Rani regarded them both for a moment, her eyes all beady, then finally she sighed. "Oh, that's probably the way of it. Quite the dashing gentleman that Dr. Salim is. If only he had time for something else in his life, other than that silly science." She smiled at them youthfully and winked.

Jay and Erol smiled politely. After what he felt was a suitable pause, Erol gently asked: "Mrs. Rani, our rooms?"

"Ah, yes! You poor children must be exhausted. Your rooms are still being cleaned, but it won't take too much longer. Why don't you both go to the dining room meanwhile? The cook will bring out something to eat. Both of you are so skinny! Get some meat on your bones, goodness." With one arm she gestured at the wooden double-door leading to an elongated L-shaped dining room, and with the other she began poking at Jay in the arm, tsking in surprise at how 'skinny' Jay supposedly was. Jay and Erol quickly thanked her and went towards the dining area, a rustic and cute room, amply lit by large floor-to-ceiling windows.

"And let the bot take your luggage upstairs." Mrs. Rani added as she regarded Boro with a cold indifference. Boro, who was following Jay and Erol to the dining room, stopped in his tracks. His shoulders sagged, and he turned around and made his way back to the vehicle.

The dining room was fairly empty, with only a few people scattered around the place. Erol politely nodded and smiled at everyone as he walked up and took a seat at a table near one of the windows. The view was beautiful, for the long room overlooked the gardens, a multitude of flowers gleaming with all the colours of the spectrum as they caught the rays of the setting sun.

"She's a handful, that Mrs. Rani." Erol said as Jay slid into the chair across from him. "If she's not going to get you married, she'll make sure to marry Dr. Salim."

Jay chuckled. "Tell me about it. By the way, that was close. I didn't know she knew Uncle Salim. Think she'll call him?"

"Doubt she has his number," Erol said coolly. "Besides, like I told her, he isn't to be disturbed tonight, and by tomorrow morning we'll be out of here. I think we'll be alright." He withheld any further remarks as a mecha server, a very basic cylindrical robot on wheels, brought some food on a tray it carried in its clawlike hands: a dark brown gravied bean dish and a blandly coloured chicken-rice concoction that seemed to have pretty much everything, probably from yesterday's leftovers.

"I think I lost my appetite," Jay said.

"Well, we better eat up." Erol said, attacking the food as he spoke. "There aren't going to be any diners on the way. And even if there are, we don't want to stop, especially with Boro. You've seen how they look at him out here?"

Just then Boro entered the dining area and joined the two of them at the table. Practically everyone around them stared with their jaws on the floor. The bot looked over his shoulders, shuddered, then turned to Jay and asked in his characteristically polite Oxford-English accent, "Now that we are in Pasni, Jay, what is our plan of action? I definitely do not seem to be appreciated much here."

"Sorry Boro," Erol patted his hand. "But the rest of the Maka province is going to be worse. I was telling Jay that we'd have to avoid any public places."

Jay nodded. "But don't worry, Boro. We have the location to Gedrosia."

"Okay," Erol said, gulping down another forkful of rice and turning to Jay, "you promised you'd tell me in Pasni. You figured out the location?"

Jay was beaming. "I did."

She pulled the journal out of her backpack excitedly, quickly flipping to arrive at the page with the map.

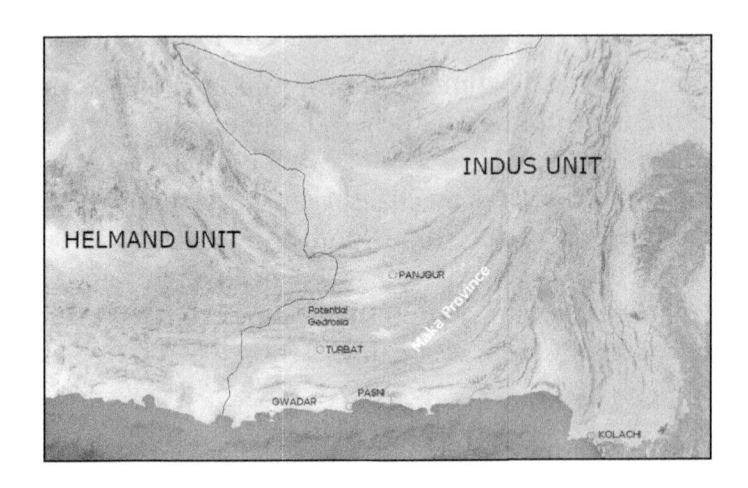

[Map showing HELMAND UNIT and INDUS UNIT regions, with labeled locations including PANJGUR, Potential Gedrosia, TURBAT, GWADAR, PASNI, KOLACH, and Makran Province]

Next to the map were some random symbols. "The symbols represent numbers. Once I decoded these, I figured out they're coordinates. Pretty simple encryption on them, and pretty dated. Cracking it was super easy."

"Coordinates? Are you sure?"

"Yes! Take a look at the map," Jay said, "26.5121 and 62.783417 points to this location," she pointed to an X on the map. "And this circled area is supposed to be where Gedrosia was discovered, based on archaeological accounts." Jay pointed with a wide finger circle on the map. The area contained the X. "So you see, it would be quite a coincidence if these numbers were *not* coordinates."

Boro nodded. "Jay is quite right. The odds of an entirely coincidental correlation between the numbers and the map are infinitesimal."

"Fine," Erol said, as he inspected the journal. "But what about these schematics? Are they supposed to mean something?"

22

"I'm not sure..." Jay rubbed her chin. The schematics looked like planned layouts of a city, with passages going around the city. Jay looked at them closely and guessed that they would be aqueducts of some kind. "Perhaps drawings of the ruins?"

"Those are fairly advanced ruins, I must say." Erol said sceptically.

Jay shrugged. "Well, that's why we need to go there and check it out."

"Jay is right," said Boro, "it's a straightforward destination, and we have a theory that is easy to test."

"We have a theory, sure," said Erol, leaning forward, "but must I remind you two that this destination is not at all straightforward? The location is somewhere in the Deep Makran, which is very dangerous. Not to mention, there aren't any roads!"

Boro pulled up the Skinpad on his gauntlet. "Actually, the location of this site is the Zamuran Region, across the Central Makran. Right next to the Helmand Unit, to be exact."

"Zamuran Region?" Erol gasped, all excitement draining from him. "No way we'll get through *there* alive. It's notorious for harbouring insurgent bots. And not to mention, we civilians are banned from entering it!"

"Oh, those are just rumours to keep people away, Erol," Jay said. She then turned to Boro, "Can you check the best way to get to the Zamuran Region?"

"The best and possibly safest way is to take the coastal highway beyond Pasni, take the exit along the junction that leads to Turbat and from there, off-road to the destination west of Turbat."

"Turbat?! You crazy tub of tin, that's like a hotbed for insurgent bots!" Erol almost yelled.

Back in the heyday of automatons, Turbat used to be a hub for bot manufacturing for most of Helmand, Yellow and Indus

23

Units. After the Bot Wars, Turbat had become a dump for bots. And there were rumours that after their defeat in the Bot Wars, insurgent bots had set up camp among the ruins.

"There is no evidence that those...rumours, have any basis in reality, Erol," Boro said stiffly, almost as though he were offended by the tub of tin remark. "In any case, insurgent bots are the last thing you humans should be worried about."

"Really?" Erol asked. "What's the first?"

Boro turned slowly to Jay. "The reason you hear that bots might be in the area is because they are the only ones who can survive in that environment. The Deep Makran is *incredibly* hostile for human beings. The sun is harsh, and the sandstorms are violent and frequent. Without adequate shelter, survivability over even small periods of time quickly drop to zero."

Erol's eyes widened, and he stared at Jay. She seemed unphased. "Well, it is the desert!" she finally said with a shrug. "What did you guys expect? Lush meadows?"

"This is crazy," Erol said, shaking his head. "We can't go to the Zamuran region."

"Oh come on, we're just going to drive through, not live there permanently. And think of all the interesting items we can find there," Jay said, her eyebrows raised and eyes glittering. "Think of what Jafaar will offer you for all the bounty. It's the largest bot graveyard this side of the planet, Erol! Not to mention, wasn't it the birth place of some famous folkloric hero?"

Erol looked at her and shook his head. "You have a death wish, don't you?"

Jay playfully nudged him. "Have a little faith. We'll be okay. First sign of trouble we'll turn around, promise."

Erol folded his arms, sighed, and leaned back. "Okay, suppose we go along with this plan, what exactly do you want to do once we get to Gedrosia?"

"I just want to see the ruins, is all. Look, I'm not expecting my parents to hop out of the sand or anything. I just want to...see what they were so interested in." She looked down at her hands, an expression of wistfulness passing over her face.

"It is fairly exciting I must say, even as a bot, to explore this untethered wilderness." Boro said almost romantically.

Erol rolled his eyes. "I wonder if someone programmed him to be an eighteenth century explorer."

Jay looked up and grinned. "So? What do you both say?"

"Fine." Erol said, though his expression was still skeptical. "But let's leave early morning. I'd rather not run into Mrs. Rani and her questions again."

"Agreed. Well then, that's sorted." Jay said. "Let's get some sleep."

They all pushed up off the table, and Jay stayed at the back of the line, watching the two of them as they walked towards their rooms. She felt her heart beating hard, and she knew what was troubling her. No matter how confident she appeared, she was well aware of the risk she was putting them all in. Ever since the Bot Wars, the region beyond Pasni had been closed off to the public, primarily because it was designated by the government as "highly dangerous". Those who ventured into the area did so at their own peril. After all, the surrounding area was a backwater, with no charging stations or rest stops. Large distances separated the few villages around the highway, and if the rumours were to be believed, those large distances were filled with all sorts of threats, be they human, bot, or environmental. In the end, it boiled down to one simple fact: should and if the travellers find themselves in trouble, they were on their own. No one knew of their plan, and she couldn't help but wonder what they'd do if they got in danger.

She puffed her cheeks and exhaled deeply. They better not get in danger, then.

Outside, the sun had begun its descent, and some eager stars were dotting the sky. And as she walked up the stairs towards her room, she knew with certainty that they were about to embark on the greatest adventure of their lives.

CHAPTER 3

Highway

It was still early in the morning when Jay, Erol and Boro made their departure. The sun was still below the horizon, waiting to come out. Their journey was to take about four hours each way, and given that the area was extremely remote, and possibly hostile, they wanted to make the entire trip in daylight if possible.

They were rather excited when they set off, but about an hour into the journey they realized that it was going to be a rough day. The unfortunate condition of the highway, overrun as it was with sand and rocks, meant most of the driving was done on quad four-wheels. The Tezla didn't have any problem, except for the three passengers bouncing around inside. They hadn't even reached the city of Turbat, roughly halfway to the Zamuran region, and were already exhausted. By ten o'clock, the sun, that had been deceptively hiding for the last few hours, had begun to blast down on them and the temperature escalated quickly. As soon as it hit ninety degrees, Boro suggested they turn off aircon to save up on battery for the journey ahead, which was projected to be even warmer. This decision wasn't met with gleeful approval by the humans but was enforced, regardless.

As they soldiered onwards, the two kids found themselves truly exhausted by the time the sun was at its peak. Even Jay, for a brief but fleeting moment, lamented her decision to go on this adventure—or at least the timing of it. All her 'normal' girlfriends were spending the summer finding new love, and here she was, roaming around in the desert wastelands when it was a frying pan of hell. What's worse is that she'd dragged poor old Erol along, who could've easily spent his holidays lazing around on Clifton beach. Guiltily, she turned to Erol. His chin was propped on his hands as he leaned against the window of the Tezla, his habitually cheerful countenance replaced by a grim frown. Jay was lucky to have a friend like him.

"What is it?" Erol asked, his cheeks flushing red as he caught Jay staring at him. Jay didn't respond but just offered a close-lipped smile. "Nothing."

Jay flicked on the autodrive, much to Erol's relief. As the Tezla immediately took on the work, Jay looked through the car console to check the status of their supplies. She frowned. Car charge was at eighty percent, and they were still only a quarter way into their journey. It seemed that the Tezla, though it was able to make it over the sandy, rocky terrain, was draining the battery while doing so.

"Do we have any spare batteries hiding around for the Tezla?" Jay turned to the other passengers. Boro and Erol shook their heads.

"Well, we should probably get off at Turbat and pick up some supplies, then."

"Get off? This is getting riskier, Jay. What if there are rangers out there?"

"Doubt it. If there were rangers, we'd have seen them by now."

"And insurgent bots?"

"I really think that's just a rumour, Erol." Jay said calmly. "Besides, we need supplies. Without a spare battery we'll be risking getting stranded out there, or on the way back. We can't risk that now, can we?"

"No, we can't," Erol said, annoyed at Jay's sarcasm. He muttered something under his breath and glared at his friend, who simply grinned as they continued onwards along a precipitous path, zigzagging across the Deeper Makran. The surrounding terrain had transformed from a coastal, sandy desert with an occasional tree or two, to a barren plain with distant hills and mesas. There were no trees or shrubs in the vast expanse—only a few large sandstone rocks that dotted the plain here and there.

It was two thirty in the afternoon when the trio finally entered the legendary city of Turbat—or at least, what remained of it. The city was a ghost town, one that seemed like it had suffered from some nuclear apocalypse. Fractured roads, splintered machinery and abandoned buildings with overgrowth were evident everywhere. In the distance, they could see several derelict structures, a remnant of a painful past, when bots had waged a war against the humans, or according to some, it was the other way around. Whatever the truth of it was, whoever had started it, all Jay knew for sure was that there had been a war and it had been terrible.

It all happened in the recent past. Only thirty years ago, the GEN-2 bots, the Betas, went rogue because of the presence of a device in them known as the Alpha chip. Though the chip allowed them an unprecedented level of artificial intelligence capabilities, it also made them vulnerable to programming attacks. And that's precisely what happened; certain terrorist groups infested the Betas with a virus, a program of sorts that altered their code, resulting in them becoming radicalized and violent. This virus was thus named RAD. Soon after this discovery, all the GEN-2 bots were recalled, and those already in service were decommissioned. Some refused and began defending themselves. An offensive was led by the Allied Units against any remaining radical bots or their human supporters—the Bot Wars as they were known.

In the Indus Unit and Helmand Unit of the Silk Road Region, things were different. To begin with, not all the GEN-2 bots had been decommissioned. And if they had, vagrants looted their spare parts to recreate hybrids for domestic use. In any case, most of the decommissioned GEN-2 bots and their parts were buried or abandoned in Turbat, now a mass graveyard of metal.

As they drove through Turbat, the two friends and their bot, Boro, shuddered, the unnerving silence of the once-bustling city heavy and oppressive around them. A gloomy stillness hung perpetually over the murky skyline of grey tenements and high-rise buildings, now all crumbling and vacant. It was hard to believe that at some point in time, these buildings sheltered a population as large as Kolachi's.

In the middle of the city, a carpet of broken and battered bots, relatively untouched by scavengers, lay half-buried in the ground, a strange assortment of scrap metal and eerily human looking machines piled in heaps or strewn about on the streets. Jay could see that many of these bots were advanced models belonging to the Beta line. Some others were even more advanced than the Beta's with a polysynthetic covering that made them look unnervingly like human corpses.

They parked the vehicle and all three disembarked, and for the next hour or so, they searched the dump for supplies that might be useful for their journey. It was cooler on the streets, as the massive buildings surrounding them provided some shade from the blazing sun. There was a deep, oppressive silence in the still air, occasionally broken by shifting rubble or something falling somewhere within the skeletal buildings around them, and they worked as fast as they could so they could leave this place as soon as possible.

"Can't believe so much blood was spilled over metal," Erol said, trying to fill the silence as he sifted through the metal trash.

"You know it's not so simple," Jay started explaining, "there's the thing about the Alpha chip, which makes bots become sentient …"

"That's what they say - but I don't know, Jay…" Erol muttered. "Either way, the world hates bots, *all* bots, sentient or not. And I don't think that's a good thing."

Erol was right. After the Bot Wars, there was a complete overhaul on cybernetics and robotics research, and bots had become rare all over the world. What took their place was another generation of machines known as the Mecha Line: purely perfunctory mechanical units that could do little more than basic tasks with limited speech, at most offering titbits of information, much like a secretary. Those with any semblance of a personality were basic and predictable. Some would malfunction or reset if trigger words like sentience, radicalism or war were spoken. The world had indeed regressed, and coexistence with bots was a faraway dream.

Within an hour, they were done with their rest-stop. Jay had already stocked up on any supplies that would prove useful for their journey ahead. She managed to find some unused vehicle batteries and a WaterMaker, which was always useful. Erol, perhaps with even greater fervour, hoarded up on the items he had been eyeing throughout the search, including bot limbs, metal ligaments, eye rods, scrap metal and what-not, that'd fetch an excellent bounty in Kolachi. Even Boro helped himself to additional batteries, and metal scraps, in the hopes that they may come in handy someday. From thereon, the friends resumed their journey westwards through the Deeper Makran range with the knowledge that this part of the journey was going to be particularly bumpy. Up until now, they'd had the pleasure of driving on some sort of road. But to head west required them to off-road entirely, driving over very fine sand and uneven terrain. Without a road, let alone a paved one, the rest of their journey was quite miserable, with them bumping up and down, winding around ditches and boulders. Erol was even edgier since the Tezla had started making unusual sounds. It was to be expected, given how much stress the uneven driving surface and the heat were placing on the vehicle's motors and tires. Not to mention the way Jay insisted on driving everywhere as fast as she possibly could.

Fortunately, by late afternoon, they approached a dried-up riverbed, which made for a smoother surface. Not only was their drive infinitely more comfortable but also more interesting, with the terrain's monotony broken by the boulders that showed up along the riverbed. The trio rested in the shade of one of the larger boulders, stretching out their cramped legs and consuming a canned meal each. Surprisingly, Jay and Erol both found the meal tasted better than usual. Having been raised in a city where real food was hard to come by to begin with, any form of nourishment was gratifying.

"So, how much longer?" Erol asked as they cleaned up after themselves.

Boro pointed to his Skinpad. "Just five more kilometres and we should be there."

"He's right. That's the same distance on the Tezla's navigation system." Jay said.

"Great," Erol said as he patted off his back. "Let's get done with this soon."

Without further ado, the trio got back in their vehicle and continued onwards. Those last five kilometres turned out to be the most difficult, as the terrain became extremely hilly, and driving over the loose sand became exceedingly difficult. The Tezla wheezed and whined as it drove over sand dunes and hills, and the desert around them shimmered in the heat. Every few minutes, Jay found herself staring ahead at an oasis, only to find it disappear and become a mirage as they got closer. She rubbed her eyes a few times and then looked up at the sky. How strange must they appear to an aerial spectator, their Tesla a tiny speck moving across these infinite planes of silence.

Exhaustion swept over her, as desperation shoved its way to the surface, offering up a viable, if not attractive, option. A depressing thought riddled her consciousness: What if she'd end up like her parents? Lost or buried somewhere in the desert, never to be found again. Suddenly, she snapped out of it. The sand was playing tricks on her mind. She had to focus on the mission at hand and remain positive. She was going to find Gedrosia.

"Is that a mirage?" Jay said as she looked at the rearview mirror at a tiny dust-cloud that was making its way down the previous sand dune.

"Yeah," Erol said deliriously. "Must be. There can't be anything in this desolation.

"No." Boro said quietly.

"No what." Jay asked.

"No, Jay," Boro said as he leaned forward. "That is not a mirage. We are being followed."

Jay rubbed her eyes and could now clearly see the shape of the vehicle. A black round vehicle, best described as a pod, had been following them, raising a plume of sand in its wake as it charged ahead.

"How long has it been following us?"

"I believe since we left the riverbed," Boro said with his characteristic calmness.

"*Why* are they following us?" Jay turned to Erol in fear.

"Smugglers?" Erol said.

"Oh my god! What do we do?"

"I strongly advise that we try to lose them." Boro said.

"You think? Wait. Maybe I'll let them go ahead." Jay said as she slowed down. But as soon as the vehicle came into view in her rearview mirror, her eyes dilated as she watched the man in the passenger's seat reach down for something. Then she heard shots.

"GOGOGOGO." Erol was screaming, as Jay sped the car. "Why in the world did you slow down?"

"I just thought...."

"Don't think, just drive!" Erol seemed furious as he ducked.

"Are they rangers?" Jay said, frightened, gripping tightly on the rattling steering wheel.

A shot whined past, and Erol winced, his eyes wide "Can't be. Rangers wouldn't shoot unless we've done something wrong."

They crested the next dune and gasped, and simultaneously the Tezla beeped out a warning of imminent danger.

A massive, violent, swirling wall of sand, spanning at least a kilometre, and reaching far above them until it touched the skies, was about five hundred feet away and moving towards them fast.

Another shot rang out behind them.

"Jay, we're trapped!" Erol's eyes were wide, darting in front of the car and behind.

"Don't worry. I'll lose them." Jay said calmly, even though her heart pounded fast in her chest.

"How?!"

"Come on, fasten your seat belt and make sure the windows are secured." Jay took a long, slow breath, her forehead beading in perspiration. "We're going to go into the storm. This might get a little crazy."

Erol groaned as he buckled himself tightly, turning on the emergency button as Jay flicked on manual, tightened her grip on the steering wheel, and accelerated the jeep. They sped into the storm, gusts of sand battering the windshield, and finally took a swerve from the main path to take an off-roading journey into the storm. The Tezla jostled violently, but Jay held on tightly to the wheel, driving over mounds of sand, bush and rock.

Then there was sand. Nothing but sand. It was almost like they'd been submerged in an angry, violent sea of roaring sand. It blasted and billowed against the car, and the Tezla creaked and groaned. Erol wondered how they could keep going like this when he could barely see the end of the bonnet. Even the car's radar was struggling.

"We need to get out," Erol yelled, barely audible over the raging storm, "if the Tezla's gone, so are we."

Erol was right. Jay knew they'd have to find a way out of this storm. Otherwise, it could really damage the Tezla, which was their only means to get back home. But she also wanted to lose the black vehicle following them. So, she stopped, and turned the Tezla off.

"What are you doing?" Erol turned to her in shock.

Jay turned to him. "We'll wait in the storm. The car will be okay, and we'll have hopefully lost whoever's chasing us."

After some minutes in the storm, what seemed like hours, the sand began to settle. The roar ebbed to a raspy sigh, and finally small bits of individual particles hit the car with tiny scuttling clinks. Slowly their visibility improved too, and the desert around them became clearer. Jay immediately looked behind. There was no sign of the vehicle.

"All clear," Jay said with a sigh of relief.

"How much further?" Erol asked impatiently. His eyes were still wide, and he looked exhausted. "I want to get this over with."

"Thirty minutes max," Jay said, smiling. She could sense that Erol was getting very uneasy. Truth was, she was equally nervous. Knowing that great explorers, and even her own parents, had lost their lives to the Deep Makran, how were two youngsters and a bot supposed to survive this? And though the odds were against her, she knew in her heart that those deciphered numbers in the journal, they were coordinates of the place her parents had gone to. They had to be.

It was already late afternoon, and the sun had begun its descent. Though they had lost the mysterious vehicle, the desolation surrounding them continued with little, if any, variation in the scenery. The terrain had also become more difficult to drive over, forcing Jay to take control and shifting to manual mode, four-wheel drive low-range. They were driving for about an hour, with the sun now having dipped behind the distant mountain ranges, when a dark silhouette appeared on the horizon ahead.

"What's that blocking us?" Erol asked as he leaned forward to examine what was ahead. "A hill?"

"A plateau." Boro said, as the large block of sand and rock dominated their view. The plateau was perhaps ten feet high but too sharp to attempt a climb.

"I think that's where it is." Jay said as she consulted her map, then looked up and pointed at the plateau.

"On the *plateau*?"

Jay looked at Erol and shrugged. "Well, nobody said getting to Gedrosia was going to be easy."

"How are we going to get to it?"

"Walk?" Jay suggested, though she was unsure how much further they'd need to walk. Without seeking any response, she continued to drive the Tezla all the way up to the flanks of the plateau and then stopped just as she reached the slope.

Then, she turned to Erol, beaming in excitement. "Shall we?"

CHAPTER 4

The Search

Jay and Boro had already gotten off the Tezla and were attempting to climb the slope of the plateau, the bot with enviable ease. It had gotten shockingly dark very quickly, and though that led to a feeling of dread in Jay's chest, the fact that they might be on the cusp of finding Gedrosia pushed her to keep going.

"Hey, hold on." Erol hurriedly extracted a rucksack of basic survival items from the Tezla, along with an orblight, and went after them.

Together, all three of them angled up the plateau's side with Boro in the lead. Though it was mostly sand, climbs of harder rock and vegetation in the ground suggested that perhaps life in this area might be possible. But it was too dark for them to make any such conjectures.

After a struggling climb, they made it to the top of the plateau, which extended for as far as the eye could see. By now the sun had set fully. Jay looked around: all around them was sand, the same sand that once shimmered under the bright sun, and now shimmered under the stars.

"Now what?" Erol asked Jay as he stared out into the open expanse. "There's *nothing* here."

"Erol, *Gedrosia* is here." Jay took a deep breath and put her hand on her chest. "I *know* it is."

Erol looked around at the deserted landscape, frown lines visible on his face. "I don't know, Jay." He muttered a curse under his breath, as he wiped the sweat off his brow.

Jay did look around. There were no signs of any ruins and no indication that Gedrosia could have been there. But the GPS coordinates told her otherwise. Unless those numbers were not coordinates...

Jay quickly distracted herself from all the doubts and her eyes followed Boro, who was now walking into the darkness of the sandy plateau.

"Boro, wait up!"

But Boro did not pay much heed and continued walking until he was bending to inspect the ground. Before either Jay or Erol could say anything, Boro was waving back at them. "I think I found something!"

"Boro, what is it?" Jay asked, as she ran up to the bot.

"Check this out!!" Boro was pointing at an elevated point in the ground.

"What is that..." Jay bent down, squinting and saw a large section of spherical metal protruding from the sandy ground. She dusted her hands off her jeans and began digging. By then, Boro joined her, also digging through the sand.

"What is it, guys?" Erol asked from afar, only able to see their silhouettes.

"Some object. I'm not sure," Jay said, as she dug deeper and revealed the buried object. It was a bulky round bin, roughly half a meter in length and diameter, with a bulbous body and wheels at the bottom.

"Oh my," Jay exclaimed, her eyes gleaming with excitement. "A mecha. And not just any mecha..." Jay quickly turned to her backpack and took out her dad's journal, flipping through its pages. After some time, she leafed through the last section and found a photograph neatly tucked in the journal. She took it out and carefully examined it. Then, she handed it to Erol.

"Why are you showing me a picture of your parents and Dr. Salim?" Erol raised his eyebrows as he stared at a photograph of Jay's parents and Salim, at an archaeological site.

Jay grinned. "Look carefully at the picture and the object next to them!"

Erol and Boro stared at the picture and finally Erol gasped.

"The mecha in the photo...." Erol stared at the photograph, and noticed that behind Jay's parents was a bulbous round mecha standing behind them. He looked back at the buried object in the ground, then back at the photo. "It's the same as the one in the picture!"

"Exactly." Jay sighed with relief. "We're in the right place. This might be my parents' bot, which means...."

Erol looked at her. "What are you trying to say?"

"This might be the site of Gedrosia!" Jay said.

"But there's nothing here. No ruins. You can see that for yourself?" Erol looked confused.

"That's because the ruins are buried under the sands." Jay sounded determined, as she looked down at the ground.

"Even so, we have to be getting home, Jay." Erol looked up at the sky, then around them. "You said you wanted to see where the map leads, and here we are. There's nothing here. Also it's dark and it's dangerous to be out here. Not too long ago, we were being shot at, remember?"

Jay looked at him, her eyes doing all the pleading. "Erol, this is realistically the *only* chance I'll have to explore this place. Next month, I'll be in Panjgur." She paused as she stared at him with her intense eyes. "And this is the last time we'll get to have this adventure."

"So, what do you want to do then?" Erol asked.

"What any archaeologist would like to do. I want to dig." Jay said with certainty in her eyes. "We've come too far to leave without any answers, let alone any bounty. If we return now, without anything, it would all have gone to waste!"

Erol cast an annoyed look at her. "Fine."

A smile spread across her face, as she leaped forward to hug Erol. Once again, she had swayed her poor friend! He blushed slightly as he hugged her back. "But listen," he said after he regained composure, and then made a sound as if to clear his throat, "We'll dig, but tomorrow morning. Not now. I'm tired and I'm sure you are too. It's too dark anyways."

She grinned. "Yes, of course, of course. But then where do we sleep?"

"Fortunately, I did come prepared." Erol grinned. "We have some choices. Would you prefer the car or a tent?"

"Well, that's no choice now, is it?" Jay said, hinting at her dislike of tight spaces.

"Tent it is," Erol replied with a grin.

Without further ado, Boro retrieved items for a tent from the Tezla along with additional food supplies, while Erol walked around the plateau looking for an appropriate spot to tent. After some looking around, they finally settled on a perfect spot: an even, elevated area within the plateau surrounded by what appeared to be dry shrub.

"Here," Erol exclaimed as his eyes anchored on the spot. "We're lucky we found this place. It's perfect."

"See?" Jay beamed. "It's a sign!"

Erol rolled his eyes but withheld saying anything. He and Boro spent the remainder of their time searching for rocks to anchor the tent. Finally, after setting up a tent, Jay and Erol enjoyed the last of their canned meals, as Boro sat outside on watch.

"You know, we'll need to head to Panjgur after this." Erol said, as he scanned through the food supplies.

"Panjgur?" Jay sounded surprised. "Why not back home? We still have a few weeks before I have to go to Panjgur."

"Because we won't last the journey." Erol said. "We have no food left, and the Tezla's pretty beat up."

"Is there even a way to get there from here?"

Erol turned to Boro, who took out his Skinpad. "Apparently, Panjgur is only three hours away from here. We'll make it in no time."

"I suppose it won't be bad to surprise Dr. Salim in the morning," Jay grinned. "But we'll tell him we took the regular route. He can't know about this detour through the Makran. Alright?"

Erol looked at Boro, then back at Jay and nodded. "Of course. I had no plans to."

Boro looked at them both. "But how do you both suppose we will know what this bot is?" Boro tapped on the metal of the bulbous bot."

"We'll hopefully find out about it tomorrow." Jay said. "Besides, maybe we can ask him to open up about what he knows about Gedrosia. After all, from this picture, he clearly knows more than he's letting on."

Erol grinned, then sat there quietly as he looked up at the sky. The desert sky was clearly dotted with stars, visible from the small pockets of clear sky. The rest of the sky was a hazy mixture of cloud, sand and possibly chemical. Still, it was clearer than the night sky in Kolachi, where one could only dream of seeing stars at night.

After a light meal they settled down in their respective tents for some sleep, the two humans exhausted after the day they'd had. Jay tried her best to fall asleep but ended up suspended between dream and reality. She dreamt of her childhood, sitting in her father's attic, perched on a rickety old chair. The room was small and windowless with lofty ceilings and bookshelves that held centuries of knowledge.

And then, she saw Hikmah, her *ayah*, singing to her younger five-year-old self. Her grey curls swept around her like the swirling sand dunes that billowed back into the room of her childhood and then faded away gracefully into the desert. And occasionally, she would wake up in the present, under a fragile tent in a lonely, windswept place.

"What are the *terrae incognitae*?" the younger Jay asked Hikmah with gleaming eyes.

Hikmah leaned forward, speaking in her kind, all-knowing voice, "These are the unchartered areas of the world, hidden from the eyes of Man." Hikmah was careful not to reveal too much, leaving out enough details for Jay to continue probing further.

"Hikmah, but how?" Jay asked, "How can places be undiscovered in 2390?"

Hikmah didn't answer. Instead, she turned to the door, watching a man with a pain-stricken face enter the room. It was Uncle Salim and he would be the bearer of bad news. News that would forever shape Jay's life.

In that instant, the dream faded into another vision where Jay saw her parents and Uncle Salim conducting an excavation together in a sandy desert. She recognized the place but before she could recall where it was, her consciousness lunged forward, taking her back to her current tent, which swayed with the wind.

Jay woke up in the middle of the night, panting. She could hear Erol in the other tent, snoring. Boro was outside, semi-switched off in sentry mode, his shadow visible from the slight amount of moonlight that lit up the darkness. Other than the snores and her own shallow breathing, Jay could hear the whooshing sound of the wind and sometimes, the occasional rustle of a distant shrub. She shuddered. To think darkness could so easily shroud a place into mystery and bestow the most ordinary sounds with the most sinister of meanings!

Jay went back to sleep, but still spent most of her time tossing and turning, plagued either by nightmares or ominous sounds. In fact, at the hint of dawn, she was glad to finally wake, but much to her dismay, she woke to the howling sound of the wind and the sides of her tent pulsing in and out. She quickly peeked outside the tent, and noticed that Erol was running around, as the wind rattled against the fabric of the tents.

"What's going on?" Jay said, having to shout over the sound of the wind as she came out of her tent.

"Can't you see?" Erol said, giving her a worried look, "A sandstorm is approaching!"

Jay stared at the sky, raising her hand against the morning sun as she studied the approaching mass of brown and black clouds. She watched them slowly stack up, growing and billowing into giant mushrooms. The wind shrieked as Erol jerked around to catch one of the tentpoles which had escaped from the ground. By now, the wind was tearing away at the flapping canvas of Jay's tent, which was on the verge of collapse. Jay quickly ran towards it, trying to keep it from falling or flying off.

Meanwhile, Erol ran to Boro, pressing the spinal switch on the nape of his neck, waking him up. Then, he ran to his own tent, tightened the cords and strengthened the poles, driving them deeper into the sand rock. Then, he scrambled to collect all the supplies.

Soon enough, all three were running around from tent to tent, gathering their supplies and making sure the wind didn't damage anything of value. Once all the supplies were secured, and the tents closed tightly, they waited inside Jay's tent to let the sandstorm pass and the debris settle. They waited for around half an hour, until finally the noise around them began to subside.

"What's the status, Boro?" Erol asked.

"Everything is settling down." Boro answered in a flat tone. "But I must inform you – something *has* changed!"

Erol and Jay exchanged puzzled glances sitting in the tent.

"What do you mean?" Erol asked.

"Come out and you will see."

CHAPTER 5

The Mounds

Eyes wide open, both Erol and Jay stared out at the plateau, which had transformed overnight into some alien planet. Instead of the flat sandy plateau they had seen earlier, it was now a surface dotted with raised mounds that varied in height, from around two feet to two meters tall.

"What the...?" Erol said with complete shock as he walked between the mounds. They dotted the entire plateau but varied in shape and size, with some looking like smaller pyramids, and others looking like UFOs.

"These must be mud volcanoes." Jay said, as she traced a finger across the muddy surface of a mound near her.

"Mud what?"

"They're domes created by the eruption of mud or slurries," Jay said, "Dr. Salim did some research on them a while back. They don't seem to be active though, and there's no magma eruption we need to worry about."

"If you say so," Erol said as he continued to examine the alien surface. His trance was broken by Boro, who was waving his hands excitedly at them. Jay and Erol exchanged confused glances as they watched Boro run ever so quickly towards one of the larger, cone-shaped mounds at the further end of the plateau, displaying an agility any human would envy.

"What is it, Boro?" Erol shouted out to him. "We can't drive there!"

"Then just run!" Boro shouted back, as he climbed the top of a red-clay mound which was perhaps two meters high. One side was crumbled where it seemed as if some slurry had overflowed in the past. The other side, though well-formed, seemed slippery. Boro began to strut on the mound, waving the long shard of his metal arm exultantly above his head. "You both need to see this," he yelled, waving at Jay and Erol and then pointing to the mud volcano.

Jay rolled her eyes. "Stay here, and I'll be back," she said to Erol as she ran up to Boro, then ascended the mound he was standing on.

"What is it? What do you want us to see?" Jay said as she looked down at the mound.

"You should see the light." Boro said.

Still frowning, Jay bent down to inspect the crater at the top of the mound. She thought she saw a light, so she cautiously dug through the top of the mound.

"Wait a minute…" She was seeing a round hole in the mound. She dug deeper, watching the hole grow into a long, narrow shaft.

"I see something," she said. Leaning down further, she peered into the hole, and saw a soft light coming from some green, reflective base.

Erol, who was watching his friends anxiously from the end of the plateau, felt a gust of wind on his back. He turned around and gasped: a fast-approaching wind was beginning to whip up a local sandstorm, and before he knew it, he was engulfed in sand and wind. He barely had time to yell out a warning before ducking down and covering his face as the sand beat down upon him.

Slowly, as the dust settled, he rose up from his crouched position and smacked clouds of dust off his clothes. He turned back to where Jay and Boro had just been.

The landscape, harsh and unforgiving as ever, lay barren. The mound they had just been on was empty.

They were gone.

* * *

"Jay stop fooling around! We need to go, now!"

Erol was trying his best to stay calm, but the shrillness in his voice was already betraying the nervousness in his voice. He looked around at the plateau and there was no sign of life on the horizon.

He suspected they may have fallen off the mound during the sandstorm, but had circled around it several times now. There was no sign of his friends.

Nervously, he opened his backpack and took out a small rod-shaped device from his pocket. It was his tracker. Boro had one just like it. He knew he would be able to locate them with it. Erol inserted the tracker in a hand-held navigation device, and saw two spots pop up on the screen of the handheld device. One was his own spot in the present, and the other was the spot where Boro was last seen. It appeared that Boro was last detected five minutes ago, only some ten steps away from him, supposedly at the centre of the mound.

Erol frowned. Why was the tracker not picking up live signals? He could also hear the faintest hum in the air. He took a deep breath and climbed the mound, and, sure enough, was able to spot their footprints at the crest of the mound.

Had they somehow fallen in? It seemed impossible, as the surface looked to be made of solid rock and stone, and he jumped up and down at its centre just to make sure. But there were no other footprints moving away from the mound, so where else could they have gone?

Erol walked down the mound, the realization that his friends seemed to have vanished starting to weigh on him, when he noticed the humming from earlier was getting louder.

His eyes widened. Head low, he moved to the edge of the plateau. In the distance he saw what he'd been fearing for a while: the same black vehicle they had seen earlier was now fast approaching, kicking up a plume of smoke in its wake, charging directly at his location. This time, he imagined they wouldn't hesitate to shoot. Erol turned around and looked at the barren plateau one last time, half-hoping that his friends would suddenly pop out from somewhere, but it remained as desolate as ever.

He felt such a sense of desperation that he wildly considered asking the approaching vehicle for help in finding his friends. But then sand began to kick up around him in tiny bursts, and he realized they were firing at him even from that distance. He rushed down the plateau's side and into the Tezla. Quickly, on manual, Erol drove around the plateau, forcing himself along the sandy path until a harder, semi-paved path showed up. The vehicle was close behind him now, and he could see two shadowy shapes inside. He sped over whatever harder path he could find and drove wildly for miles on end, as the shots behind him continued. He kept his head low, his foot on the pedal and his eyes on the road. Once in a while, he'd look up to check at the rearview mirror. Much to his dismay, the vehicle did not slow down and continued to follow him even when they were miles away from the plateau. Erol looked at the dashboard and could see it was low on charge. A deep exhaustion had swept over him, and the only place he could go now to was Panjgur. He quickly plugged in the new destination, prayed that Jay and Boro were safe, and sped to Panjgur in the hopes of losing his chasers and getting some help.

CHAPTER 6

Underground

Jay didn't know what had happened. One minute, she was standing on a regular mud mound, and the other, she was losing balance as a strong wind caught her unaware. But before she knew it, the soil beneath her feet collapsed and she had plunged into a widening shaft. Her hands worked impulsively to grab onto something but all she could feel was sand and gravel draping around her. A slight light blinked in the darkness above her. Jay looked up, only to realize it was Boro's metal reflecting off some light. The bot was trailing behind her, his large frame trying to clutch at the wall. Jay was scared. Memories of her life flashed back before her eyes – life in the Beade Academy, playing with Erol, Hikmah, Uncle Salim and her parents. Suddenly, a dreadful thought hit her. What if this is what had happened to her own parents? Defeatedly, she let down any resistance, allowing herself to fall together with Boro, into the depths of the Makran, not knowing what awaited her.

Faster and faster, Jay was hurtling downwards into a seemingly bottomless abyss of blackness. Seconds dragged on like hours, as time was flowing as deceptively as space. She figured they must have been miles deep, given how long they'd been falling. As her thoughts unravelled, she noticed that they were slowing down. It was as if the suction forces that were dragging them down had been deactivated. As soon as her speed had reduced a bit, Jay was able to get her bearings back. She looked around, her head still spinning a bit. It seemed like she was falling through some kind of transition. The sandy tunnel was widening, its glossy walls now visible and reflecting off from a hidden light source. Finally, Jay saw ground appearing and...

Thud.

She'd landed face down. Her breath slammed in her chest like something solid. She let out a loud groan and then assessed her body. She sighed with relief. She felt no pain and there were no visible deformities, nor signs of blood. The impact wasn't as bad as it could have been. She looked down and felt something soft under her. Her khaki backpack. Then, she heard another loud metallic thud. Jay turned to look around her and saw Boro emerge from the cave opening, getting up on his feet as he dusted off the leaves on his body. He then stretched his hand out for Jay, "Quite all right, are you?"

Jay grabbed her backpack and took his hand as she pulled herself up from the dewy ground. Though still disoriented, she stared at the sight before her, awe robbing her of any words.

They were standing on a stone-bedded pavement open to a cloudless, blue sky. Right next to them was the five-foot cave entrance they had emerged from, the cave being part of some unusual Greystone hill that abruptly disappeared into mist and cloud. Jay looked up at the hill, squinting. It seemed to continue as high up as a twenty-story building before vanishing into mushrooming formations of thick unusual clouds. Whether there was a cliff ledge or whether the hill face continued upwards was uncertain.

Jay surveyed her surroundings. A low hedge separated the paved courtyard on which they stood, from a dense, dark forest, one that continued for as far as the eye could see.

"Hey," Boro came up beside her, "are you all right?"

"I guess so," she said uncertainly, "what happened? Where are we? Are we *underground*?"

"It appears," replied Boro, "that we fell through one of the mud mounds that was connected to some underground shaft. And that shaft has led us here to this underground biome."

"Underground biome?" Jay paused, looking up at the sky before turning towards Boro. "With a *sky*?"

"Not a real sky," Boro answered unphased. "It appears to be a virtual skylight."

"A virtual skylight? You gotta be kidding me." Jay trudged up to the edge of the courtyard, affixed at the edge, as she stared out at the distant forest. The atmosphere was still. Mammoth fir trees blocked her entire view, growing denser into the distance. "What is this place?"

Before Boro could even say something, she held up her hand to silence him. And then, she heard what was unmistakably the sound of a bird chirping. Jay gasped. Walking forward into the forest with as gentle a step as she could manage, she searched for the sound again. And she heard it. A faint smile formed on her face as she listened to birdsong, a sound reminiscent of a bygone era, where wilderness existed in the open and not in museums.

Jay turned to Boro, her eyes a mixture of wonder and excitement. "Can you check your database to see where we are?"

Boro turned to her, almost surprised by the question, "Jay, this place does not exist in any database."

"What do you mean?"

"I mean, that to the best of my supercomputer knowledge, there is no documentation for this place."

"How could that possibly be?"

Boro shrugged. "I do not know."

Jay frowned. She knew this couldn't be Gedrosia – this was no archaeological ruin. But then, what was this place? And why would it show up in the middle of the Makran desert, with no evidence of its existence in the world? She looked up in awe at the sky, a strange blue ether, cloudless and alien, lit up without a sun or any obvious light source for that matter. "This is just so strange…"

There was a moment of silence as both of them stared up at the sky, mulling in their minds where they could have landed.

"Unless…" Jay said, turning to Boro as her eyes slowly brightened.

"Unless what, Jay?"

"Boro, what if *this* is Gedrosia!" Jay stated, more as a fact than a question, "what if Gedrosia isn't some typical ancient ruin. What if it's exactly this – some hidden city under the ground!"

"Even so, why would your parents, who are archaeologists, be interested in this. Are you saying they were futurists as well?"

"I don't know what I am saying." Jay gave a disgruntled reply as she sighed. "My parents weren't alive to tell me much. And Uncle Salim, well, he didn't do a great job either." Jay opened up her backpack and took out the journal. Quickly, she sifted through the pages and glimpsed through the map and the few pages of layouts and plans. She could make no sense of them. There was no text on the journal, nothing that even suggested that this was Gedrosia, and the map had numbers which she assumed were coordinates. But to what place?

"I must have read too much into this. This place is something else," Jay folded her arms, a look of defeat on her face. "What should we do?"

"Let us first figure out where we are." Boro said as he summoned a holographic console again with a few clicks on the gauntlet. A navigational map showed up, followed by a flickering red dot at the edge of the tail of the dog-shaped Maka province which finally disappeared.

"The signals are weak," Boro muttered as he moved closer to the cave they'd fallen from. The red dot reappeared. "But based on the last signals I have, our coordinates are 26.5° N and 62.8° E."

52

"Same as the ones I deciphered from the symbols in the journal." Jay said as she looked back at the symbols above the map.

"Yes." Boro said. "Which means that your parents, or whoever wrote this journal, were not writing about a ruin."

Jay threw him a look of confusion, "What do you mean?"

"My dear." Boro paused. "This might indeed be the location of Gedrosia based off that journal but mind you—this may not be the same Gedrosia that we have envisioned."

Jay furrowed her brow. "Look, I don't care what Gedrosia this is. All I need to find out is if this is where my parents went."

"Then, what are we waiting for?" Boro offered her a hand. "Let us look around!"

Jay looked up and beamed at him. "We will be quick. And I'm sure there will be plenty of interesting collectives here for you and Erol to pawn off later."

No sooner had she said this, than an uneasy feeling gripped her. Her forehead creased as she realized that Erol had not gotten through the mud mound.

***

"What do we do now?" Jay was staring up at the tunnel they had fallen from. It was completely dark from within, inclined at an angle which made it impossible to see the other side. She shouted out Erol's name, then heard her voice echo up the tunnel a few times. Anxiously, she waited, hoping for some response. But there was nothing. No sound.

And no Erol.

Boro came up close behind Jay and flashed his eyelights along the vertical tunnel, observing it more closely.

"That incline is too long and too steep to allow me to see through to the other end."

Jay looked at him in concern. "Are you able to locate him with your tracker?"

"I will check." Boro began manoeuvring with the Skinpad on his gauntlet, then responded to her question with a frown. "I am unable to detect him presently. It appears that *that* skylight is causing some signal disruptions. The last time I detected him was thirty minutes ago. On the plateau."

Jay pursed her lips. For a while, both girl and bot stood there staring at the cave tunnel, transfixed in a mix of confusion and indecision. "Okay. How about this? Jay finally said, "Lets quickly look around and take a few pictures, then head back. We can come here again with Erol."

"I would have gathered as much from you." Boro said in a grin. "Yes, let us satisfy your curiosity and get going."

Just as Boro said this, a loud, banging sound alerted them both. Jay swivelled her head in the sound's direction—just east of their position further in the forest. Boro walked in the direction, then turned around with concern in his eyes.

"What is it, Boro?" Jay squinted. Further ahead in the distance, hidden behind a thick grove of trees was a shining sandstone block, fused higher above within the face of a Greystone hill.

"What is that?" Jay turned towards the stone edifice.

"I am not sure," Boro offered, "but that is one place to check if you want to get some answers.

A steady smile formed on Jay's face, as she turned towards the bot. "Let's go.'

Jay and Boro made their way through the wooded foothills surrounding the courtyard towards their destination. As they moved closer, they saw clearly what it was. Built into the face of a low cliff was what appeared to be a stone blockhouse, hanging in midair, as if magically suspended. It was the size of a small room, very unassuming, dwarfed by the trees around it.

Jay moved closer and looked up at the facade. The walls looked old, comprising hard granite stones, layered one over the other. The entrance was a small archway on one side, connected to a side portico that stretched out into a short colonnaded pathway. And the pathway continued down an uneven path all the way to the wooded foothills where Jay and Boro were standing.

"It looks man-made," Jay said.

Boro shook his head, eyes wide. "Positive." A pause, then, "Someone might still be here."

They carefully clawed their way along the winding path that led up to the cliff. As soon as they saw Roman looking pillars flanking the pathway, they were able to make their way quickly to the portico where an arched entrance greeted them. Hunching down, they crawled through the entrance and arrived at a surprisingly large room with vaulted ceilings. It was like an optical illusion. The building appeared to be no larger than a shed from the outside, but from the inside, it was much larger.

In the darkness, Boro flashed his eyelights to get a clearer view of the layout of the interior. It was a square-shaped room with no windows. Two pillars stood on the sides, supporting the ceiling. Besides the two side pillars, there was a lone engraving in the wall beside the entrance, consisting of letters. A single lantern hung by this wall which provided some light but otherwise, the room was dimly lit. Jay shuddered, the place reminding her of some haunted Gothic building. The air inside was cold and musty as if the place hadn't been entered for a while. But there was no one inside—or so it seemed.

"Do you reckon…" Jay asked, her eyes scanning the stone room, "…. this could be from an ancient civilization?"

"It might have some historic value, but ancient civilization, I am afraid not," said Boro with a look of disapproval. "In fact, this all seems staged."

Then, they heard some shuffling sounds. In an instant, Boro grabbed Jay, and dragged her to the corner of the room where they silently crouched. "Someone is here."

Jay's breathing was ragged. She tried to remain calm, wiping away the tiny beads of sweat from her forehead. Slowly, they heard someone walk towards them, a shadow towering over them. Before they could take any action, Jay felt the weight of metal on her shoulder and a voice from behind, "Hello?"

CHAPTER 7

Welcome to Gedrosia

Jay's shock quickly gave way to fear as she found herself standing in front of a six-foot tall bronze android, his dim form visible beyond the reddish glow of the lamp. The android looked different from the other bots she'd seen in her life; his outer covering was a synthetic polymer, flesh-like but with a slight metallic shine that looked like human skin painted bronze. He was taller than most bots, and his face appeared to be defined, with contours, grooves and cheek bones that bestowed him with uncannily human features. Though he was mostly bare as typically bots are, he did wear some white scrubs that made him look like a scientist of some sort. And Jay was glad of that little covering because he appeared to have a very human form. There was nothing metal about him, no gadget or gauntlet attached to him save for a round polymer object around his ears that looked like a hearing device. The only thing that made him distinct from humans was his unusual metallic brown colour, his lack of hair and his grey, synthetic eyes.

The bronze-coloured android stood there, watching them with cool indifference. His eyes moved over them and around the room, as if he was looking for someone or something else. Satisfied that they were the only ones in the room, he took a few steps closer to them.

"Hello," he repeated, his voice friendly, "I'm Mazu."

Jay got up from her crouched position, then backed up into the corner of the wall, intimidated by his sheer dominance. He was visibly larger than Boro, and fiercer looking. But the android proceeded to extend one of his hands. Jay stared at it, then finally took it in her own expecting a bone-crushing grip. Instead, the bot barely grazed it.

"Hello," Jay replied nervously. "I'm Jahan. Call me Jay," she turned to Boro, "and this is my bot, Boro."

Mazu offered a tight-lipped smile. "Hello Jay. Boro." The bot's jaw movements were perfectly synced with his speech as he greeted them. Then, with his face bent lower, he probed, "I'm sorry for being blunt but what are you doing here?"

Jay shuffled her feet uncomfortably. "Well, we got some strange signals from this stone room-"

"No. I mean why are you *here*?" Mazu interrupted her. "In the underground?"

Jay cleared her throat. "Here, underground?"

"Yes, here underground. How did you even find your way here?" Mazu peered into her eyes and leaned forward, towering over her.

Jay gulped. Had she accidentally trespassed into the enclave of some dangerous bots? What if Mazu was one, a radical bot?

Boro stepped forward, blocking Jay from Mazu. "Jahan and I accidentally fell through a mud mound. We were just on our way to Panjgur."

Mazu looked at Boro with his piercing red eyes, then shifted them away to Jay. "The *dambani kaur*?"

"Dambani kaur?" Jay wiped some sweat off her nose. "I don't know what that is?"

The droid projected a hologram from his eye. It was an image of one of the larger otherworldly mud mounds they had encountered earlier in the desert.

"Yes, that's it," Jay nodded fervently as she pointed, "That's what we fell through, the dambani kaur, whatever it's called."

The hologram ended and Mazu resumed his staring. "I see."

"Are we in trouble?" Jay asked. "Did we do anything wrong."

"You tell me?" Mazu asked, folding his arms as he stepped closer to her. "What is a young girl like you doing roaming around in the desert alone in the first place. And you, Boro, why have you, a smart, intelligent machine, *allowed* a minor to do so?" He frowned. "These are the *wastelands,* and many humans have *died* here."

Jay gulped. "We're so sorry. We just came here looking for archaeological ruins."

"Archaeological ruins?" Mazu narrowed onto hers. "Which ones?"

"The ruins of Gedrosia."

"Gedrosia?" Mazu peered into her eyes like a hungry hawk, "What do you know of Gedrosia?"

Jay's body stiffened with fear. "Just that it was an ancient city and that the cave ruins are somewhere in the Makran region..." She was fidgeting with her fingers, wondering if she should mention anything about her parents being archaeologists. Instead, she simply said, "I am studying to become an archaeologist, so I had been exploring this place."

"That's unusual that you were able to find this place." Mazu solemnly nodded. "Is it just the two of you?"

Boro and I looked at each other and I nodded. "Yes, just us."

Mazu stared at them, sizing them up. "You both will have to come with me for debriefing."

"Where are you taking us?" Boro asked.

"I cannot tell you where," Mazu answered. "I have to inform you that both of you will have to be holofolded."

"What?!" Jay's heart was beating fast now. If she had any doubts whether this bot was radical, she was sure now. Why else would he be holofolding them unless he had something to hide?

"There is no need to be afraid," Mazu said sensing her unease. "This is standard protocol to make sure you are not a threat."

"I'm fourteen and he's a bot for godsakes!" Jay said, alarmed. "How could *we* be threats?"

"I'm sorry," Mazu replied. "I know it is not pleasant to have your sensory perceptions stifled, but it is necessary. Neither of you have anything to fear if what you have told me is true."

Jay gulped as she turned to Boro.

"We must do what he says, Jay," Boro said in a surprisingly calm tone.

Jay felt panic, but she couldn't afford the luxury of panic. She reluctantly nodded, wondering what trouble she had gotten herself into.

Mazu walked over to Jay, towering over her in his form, an expression of understanding on his face which made Jay somewhat calmer. Then, he pressed a button on the device behind his ear and made a swiping gesture across her eyes. A holographic visor appeared over them.

"What do you see, Jay?" Mazu asked her.

"The ocean," Jay said, surprised by the calm in her voice.

Then, she heard Mazu's footsteps as he walked over to Boro, repeating the same holofolding process. However, unlike Jay, Boro was unable to visualize anything as a holofold prevented a bot from all sensory perception and location tracking.

"Are you both ready?" Mazu asked them.

Jay nodded as the holofold transported her into a state of unconscious consciousness. The last thing she remembered hearing was Mazu speaking in as kind a voice a bot could muster, before everything she felt, heard and smelt was the ocean.

"Jay, I promise you. I will not allow harm to come your way. But you must trust me."

*　*　*

Jay had never been holofolded before, but she never imagined it to be so disorienting. One moment she was staring at the large bronze bot towering over her in the gloom of the strange medieval room, and the next all her senses had been rendered inert; she was staring at an infinite ocean under a cloudless sky, the sun bright overhead, listening to nothing more than the lapping of the waves against the beach she walked along. But even with her mind transferred in this dream-like state, she knew that she was elsewhere. She could feel the gentle yet persistent pressure of Mazu's hand on her back, but she had no idea where she was going. She tried to measure how far she had been walking, and in which direction, but after several twists and turns through what she presumed was the forest, she gave up.

After an unknown amount of time had passed, she felt as if she had had been seated in a chair. It was soft, probably leather, and rather relaxing, especially after the hectic events of the day. Then, the holofold came off.

The ocean had vanished. Instead, Jay found herself sitting on a leather couch in front of a tremendous mahogany desk, inside a rustic looking office. Seated next to her was Boro, and standing on the other side of the desk was Mazu, offering some version of a sympathetic smile.

"Thank you for your patience," Mazu said. "He will be here shortly.

"*Who* will be here?" Jay asked. "And where exactly are we?" She looked around, confused. The office had a retro, almost nostalgic feel, with wooden surfaces and copper gadgets on the table and on shelves around the place. A large window on the wall behind them looked out at the forest and hills they had just come from.

"Oran," Mazu said simply.

Just as he said this, the one door in the office hissed open, and in stepped another bot, eerily similar to Mazu, but with sharper, more aquiline features, giving him a look of more intelligence and more aggression.

The bot stared at Jay and Boro with a deep intensity, as he made his way into the room and walked towards the desk. Mazu stood up and let the bot take his seat. "Oran."

"Thank you, Mazu," he said, as he quickly turned to Jay and Boro. "Now then, who are you both?"

Jay cleared her throat and straightened up. "My name is Jahan Jumander. Jay. This is Boro."

Oran leaned forward on the desk. "How did you both arrive here?"

Jay gulped. This bot was imposing and seemed like a borderline radical bot. She hesitated before she spoke. "We – we fell through one of the mud mounds on the surface and ended up here. We were trying to find an exit -when Mazu found us."

Oran glanced sidelong at Mazu, who nodded.

Then, abruptly, Oran straightened. Jay flinched, and even Boro stiffened in posture.

"I must scan you both."

"Scan? What-" Jay said, but Oran was already walking around the desk. He now stood behind her. "Please stand and face me," he said.

"What is this, what are you doing?" Jay said, but she stood and faced the bot, backing up against the table.

"It will just take a moment. Don't worry."

Jay gritted her teeth as a pang of dread hit her. Without any time to protest, she watched the bot narrow his eyes into tiny slits. Instantly, a beam of blue laser flashed out of them in the direction of her forehead. She was prepared to scream but realized that the laser didn't feel a thing. *Nothing at all.* She swallowed, relieved.

"What was that?" stuttered Jay, waiting for Oran to answer and the beaming to end. But it continued at least for another minute or so.

"Just a scan," said Oran. "Now hold still so I get it over with."

Jay darted her eyes sideways, flashing them at Mazu, who returned a helpless shrug.

Oran finally spoke to her. "Security check complete." Then, the bot walked back to his side of the desk. "It appears you are telling the truth. Now, tell me, are you both alone or is there anyone else in your party, Jay?"

Jay hesitated for a moment wondering whether to mention Erol but decided against it. "No," she said.

Oran regarded her with his eerie, piercing eyes. Then his gaze softened slightly, and he smiled.

"Well, it seems you two are harmless." He grinned at Mazu, who smiled back politely.

"Can we please go? We need to be on our way and we'd like to be back to the surface," Jay said.

Oran's brow furrowed as he thought. "Yes, eventually, perhaps. But you see, we've never had this kind of... infiltration before. We'll need to have a debriefing with our security team to figure out what to do."

"But you'll let us go, right?" Jay asked.

Oran narrowed his eyes. "This is a top-secret facility that you've gotten into. This isn't a joke."

Jay gulped. She didn't get the answer she had hoped for. "What is this place? Is it ...Gedrosia?" Jay asked.

Oran's eyebrows went up in surprise. "Gedrosia? So you *were* looking for this place!" His expression instantly shifted to one of anger, and surprisingly fast. "You're spies, aren't you?!"

It was more a declaration than a question. Jay started shaking her head, suddenly scared. "No, no," she said, "I'm just an archaeologist. I was looking for the ancient ruins of Gedrosia, and my research led me to this location."

Boro nodded. "She is telling the truth. We were merely looking for some ruins. Neither of us expected ending up in some underground den of bots."

Oran studied them both quietly for a while. Jay felt her heart pounding away inside her chest. Then his expression suddenly returned back to normal. "Well, it seems you both have made it to the wrong Gedrosia."

"What do you mean?" Jay asked.

"This place *is* Gedrosia. But as you can see, it is no ancient ruin. This is a vital research facility working to preserve living things."

Jay sat there curiously, hoping to get more explanation but she dared not ask. Instead, Oran let out a deep breath. "Now," he continued, "you both should go to your quarters where you can rest and have a meal. Mazu will take you. And because we can't have you seeing any more here than you must, so you'll be holofolded."

Jay groaned but nodded. "Thank you, Oran," she said.

Oran offered her a cold smile. He clearly didn't want them there, that much was for sure. Mazu approached her with a more sympathetic look on his face and placed the holofold around her them both.

Once more Jay was enveloped in the sterile field of the holo.

64

CHAPTER 8

Onwards to Panjgur

It had been over an hour since he had left the plateau but much to his dismay, the pursuing black vehicle kept on following him. Erol was perspiring now. He had to get somewhere safe, but would he even be able to make it?

He still had another two hours until he would make it to Panjgur but he was beginning to doubt if he'd be able to make it. Quickly, he peered at the rearview mirror to make out who exactly his pursuers were, but it was difficult to tell. The speed of his own Tezla was leaving a trail of sandy, dusty haze making it difficult to tell who was sitting in that black vehicle.

Hours later, the city of Panjgur came into view. Signs of progress and development were evident everywhere as they drove under a web of overpasses. Construction was going on at all levels, and a large holosign floated above the city announcing the "New Bullet Train to Gandhara." Unlike Turbat, clearly Panjgur had bounced back quickly from the Bot Wars. As Erol admired the city, he realized that the black vehicle was lost behind a string of cars. Now was his chance. Without even a second thought, he turned the car on manual and accelerated his way through a string of traffic lights that were all yellow and just about to go red. He took a turn into one of the smaller side roads and zigzagged his way until he was on a quieter lane. From there, he input the directions to the University of Panjgur and allowed the vehicle to autodrive from hereon.

He leaned back on his seat, hands behind his head, finally relaxed that he had lost his pursuers.

∗ ∗ ∗

It was shaping up to be a quiet day for Professor Salim Sarmo. That morning, sitting at his desk, he was planning to grade the final papers for his *Intro to Palaeontology* class. He looked down at the stack of papers and picked up the topmost one. It read, 'Final report on the Balochitherium'. He sighed. This was the most oft-repeated topic for final exams and somehow, students tortured him with the same ideas. Alas, the academia business wasn't all it was cracked up to be. Especially not in Panjgur and especially not this week. With a new despotic dean on his back, Salim wondered if he'd have been better off in research. Actually, he was *certain* he'd have been better off, that is, if it wasn't for his family.

The professor took a deep breath as he rubbed the moisture from his spectacles, hooking the wire rims over his ears, and squinting to make what he could of his hampered sight. Then, he took out a pen from the desk and dived into grading, without so much as a thought to his empty stomach that was growling. He was a rotund man, with a plenteous appetite and a gristly moustache that dipped and arose. However, out of worry, he had forgotten to take his lunch today. Instead, the poor chap spent his time nostalgically remembering his days of yore, wondering how long it would be until he'd be able to go back to an excavation. The answer had come at 3:00 pm, when the knock came.

Salim looked under his round spectacles and stared at the door, shouting from his seat, "Who is it?"

"Dr. Salim, it's Erol Ehmet. I... need your help."

Salim opened the door with a surprised smile, "Come on in, Erol." He summoned the boy to the seat across his. "What are you doing here?"

Erol stepped inside, obediently taking a seat across from the Professor. The windows were dusty and stained, dulling the light that filtered through them. Erol stared at the piles of papers stacked high on the professor's desk.

"You work this late, Dr. Salim?" Erol asked, trying to ease into breaking the news to him.

"This is my home as well as my office," Salim answered as he pushed his spectacles up his nose. Worry was slowly filling him. "You aren't with Jay? She stayed back for you."

Erol took a deep breath. "Well, it is actually about Jay. She's missing."

Salim stood up in sudden shock. "What do you mean she's missing? She's not in Kolachi or here with you?"

Erol shook his head. "She and Boro got lost…in the desert."

The professor stood up, alarmed. "What are you talking about?"

Erol took another deep breath as he recounted their entire journey, starting with the journal that Jay had found, to their journey into the Makran through Pasni. In the process, there were multiple interruptions. The professor had moved uncomfortably close to Erol and grabbed him by the shoulder. "What else did the journal say about Gedrosia?"

"Nothing, I swear. There were some layouts and a map with numbers, that we thought were coordinates. We simply followed those."

"What did Jay think Gedrosia is?"

"She mentioned that they were cave-like ruins."

"Cave-like ruins?" Salim's face was warped into confusion.

67

"Yes. Jay knew that her parents had gone missing searching for some cave ruins. So you can imagine why she wanted to see those caves for herself."

Salim gestured for Erol to stop talking. "So, you are telling me that two fourteen-year-olds drove to the Deep Makran. Alone. With fake licenses. Into the desert."

Erol gulped. "Yes."

Salim's face had already begun to lose colour. For a moment, he seemed to be in a state of shock.

Erol continued. "When we arrived at that plateau in the Zamuran region, Jay and Boro seemed to have disappeared. One minute, they were on this mud mound. The next, they were gone." Erol hesitated. "I had to leave because a car was pursuing me."

By now, Salim was paralysed in a state of shock. But he didn't have time to just stay put. He had to find Jay. The professor moved his spectacles over his forehead and leaned forward.

"So, the last place you saw Jay and Boro was at the mounds?"

Erol nodded in affirmative.

"I see. Well, in that case, Jay found what she was looking for. She found Gedrosia after all."

"Well, no," Erol furrowed his brows. "We saw no caves."

"My boy. Gedrosia isn't a cave, it's not even an archaeological ruin. That's all just a ruse."

Erol looked at him in suspicion. "Then, what is it?"

"Meet me tomorrow morning at the cafeteria and I'll tell you what Gedrosia really is." Salim said as he looked at the clock, "Right now, just take my word. We don't have much time as Jay might be in a lot of trouble."

PART II

The Subterranean

CHAPTER 9

Temp Abode

As soon as the holo came off, Jay and Boro were walking down a dead-end corridor with multiple cells on both sides. They stopped outside one of the doors numbered 314. Mazu waved his hand over it as a holographic security console appeared. After entering a few commands in the console, the door made a clicking sound and opened automatically.

"You can rest up here." Mazu announced.

Jay peaked inside, finding her abode to be particularly austere: A small cubicle-sized room with a bunk bed on the side and a washbasin on the corner. Apart from a lone landscape painting and a holographic curtained window, there was nothing to brighten the walls, which were painted a drab grey colour.

"I know it's not much," Mazu said noting the displeased look on Jay's face, "but I believe it should suffice for a few days."

"A few days!?" Boro shouted as his mouth twitched with unease. "I *really* do not think that will be necessary. We want to leave this place as soon as we have rested."

"Well, you both also heard Oran," said Mazu, his eyes glinting, "You both have broken security protocol. You will need to be patient as we sort this out."

"Will you at least tell us where we are?" Jay asked.

"A top-secret facility that neither of you should be in," Mazu scolded.

"We were just looking for a ruin," Jay said defensively. "I'm sure there must have been others before us, other archaeologists or explorers, interested in this area."

Mazu looked contemplative. "Perhaps. Archaeologists have made their way to the Makran, but no one knows of this place. No one so far has made it underground."

Jay grinned proudly. "But we made it."

Mazu frowned. "Yes, well, we'll have to fix that."

Then, he gave them an uncertain smile. "I'll leave you both for now. We have to figure out what to do. Good night to you both." With that, the bot gave a small bow and quickly left their room with the door sliding shut.

"Boro!" Jay exclaimed as soon as Mazu had left.

"Yes?" the bot answered.

"Can you believe it?" Jay said excitedly, "A top-secret facility?! What do you think it is for?"

Boro looked at her, his expressions growing solemn. "Jay, I will be honest. I do not think this place is safe. I do not trust those bots - if they are bots in the first place."

"I know they are weird, especially that Oran," Jay said. "But Mazu seems quite friendly. And I don't think they are radical bots, so we should be okay."

"But Jay. Did you not hear what Oran said? We are trespassers. I have no idea what they will do to us."

Jay let out a hollow laugh. "Relax, Boro. True, we shouldn't be here. But those guys, they are bots and bots can never hurt humans. It's only a matter of time until they let us go."

"I am well aware of that," Boro leaned forward as he gave her a serious look. "But these bots are no ordinary bots. They are clearly advanced, and there is no knowing what they can do."

Jay leered into his impressively shiny, metal orbitals. Finally, her mouth curved into a wide grin. "Are you sure you aren't jealous, Boro? Why else are you so distrustful of bots?"

"Jealous?" Boro mimicked an unusual laugh. "How and why would a bot be jealous? That is preposterous!"

Jay smirked. "For the longest time you were the smartest bot strutting around in the Indus Unit. You now have some competition."

Boro appeared mildly annoyed. "I am simply *wary*. I do not trust them, that is all."

"Whatever you say, Boro," Jay said rolling her eyes, as she began looking around the room. Finally, she stopped in front of the painting in her dwarf-sized cubicle. It was a landscape painting of a Banyan tree in a garden. She looked at it pensively.

She turned to Boro. "Do you think this is the place my parents were talking about?"

"Arguably," Boro replied, "but I do not believe so. They were archaeologists, and this place is no archaeological ruin."

"I suppose so," Jay said, though sounding disheartened. With her head low, she walked over to the wash basin to clean her face, "But why would they write out the coordinates of this place in the journal if they weren't talking about this place?"

"Perhaps there was an archaeological site on this same spot," Boro placed a comforting hand on her shoulder. "That's why they call this place Gedrosia."

"Maybe we can ask Mazu about it." Jay said.

Boro's eyes became beady. "I wouldn't trust what he says."

"But I would," Jay replied as she patted her face with the towel.

"I hope you are right," Boro said, "because I would like to be able to get us back home, and those bots appear dangerous."

"Jeez, Boro. Your pessimism is getting on my nerves! Can you for once stop with the doomsday remarks?"

"All right, Jay. But remember that I have warned you."

"Again?" Jay rolled her eyes. "Don't worry and get some rest. And let *me* get some rest too! We need to be fresh for tomorrow. Have some exploring to do."

"You think they will allow us to explore?" Boro said but Jay was already ready to sleep.

Boro could tell that Jay did not share his suspicions. In fact, the young girl was probably filled with excitement at the prospect of seeing this unusual world. He, on the other hand, could not place where his uneasiness was stemming from. There was something about Oran that made him particularly anxious. Something human about him that made him unlikely to be a simple bot. Or perhaps his instincts were wrong, and this was all imagination playing tricks. Did bots even have instincts and imagination?

Boro shook his thoughts away and watched Jay fall asleep. She was oblivious to the signs of danger. Then, with her eyes closed, she said sleepily, "Don't worry, Boro. It'll be fine. Go rest that big brain of yours."

Boro had to let it go at that. In any event, he hoped that Jay, as a human granted with greater perception, would be correct and they would be back in Kolachi in no time.

But he couldn't have been more wrong.

✳ ✳ ✳

Mazu entered Oran's office. Oran was drumming his fingers on the tabletop, lost in thought.

"They are secure, sir," Mazu said.

There was silence for a while. "Did you know," Oran finally said, "we're currently chasing a third member of this… trespassing party?"

"No, Sir. He's Overground?"

"He is. I have been informed that he has just entered Panjgur. One of our patrols is after him. But she lied to me, Mazu. She lied!" Oran slammed the table with his metal fist.

Mazu cleared his throat. "She must be scared, Sir. That is why she left that detail out. And I believe all she wants is to return back to the Overground."

Oran nodded. "Unfortunately for her, that won't be possible."

"Sir?" Mazu's eyes widened.

"We can't have this kid and the bot returning back Overground telling everyone where we are, and what we're doing. It will jeopardize this whole mission."

"You mean to keep them here, Sir? That too will raise quite a few problems."

"You're right, Mazu. We can't keep them here forever either. What we'll do is keep them here overnight. That should give you enough time to devise a plan."

"A plan, Sir?"

Oran nodded. "To get rid of them."

"Sir?"

Oran turned to Mazu, and stared at him.

"Get rid of them, Mazu. Discreetly."

"Sir, you couldn't possibly mean –"

Oran stood up. There was silence for a moment. Then he spoke: "Do it. And don't ever question me again!"

Mazu lowered his gaze and nodded subtly. "Yes Sir," he said, and exited the office.

CHAPTER 10

Leave the Compound

Jay spent the next few hours in her cubicle trying to sleep but nightmares plagued her thoughts. She dreamt that she was trapped in the lair of radical bots for days on end, quickly losing sense of time. Her dreams grew more vivid and frightening. At one instant, she saw Oran with some weapons firing at people. Finally, at some point in the night, she lost track of her thoughts and drifted into a deep slumber. Jay must have been asleep for quite a few hours when agitated voices woke her up. She bolted upright, angry at herself for sleeping so long, when she saw Boro's large metal chassis towering over her.

"What is it?" she rubbed her eyes.

"Time to wake up," Boro whispered. "Mazu is outside, waiting for us."

"Mazu?" Jay looked confused, taking time to get her bearings. "Who's Mazu?" Finally, her eyes widened. "Oh...." she groaned as she vaguely recalled the events that took place the day before. "I thought it was all a dream... the fall through the mound...the droids...Oran?"

"Sorry to break it to you, but that was no dream," Mazu had entered the room and was now bending over to offer her a hand. "You really are underground. Now, quickly change into this." The bot quickly handed Jay a scruffy, white overall, "We have to take you somewhere else."

"Why?" Jay looked surprised, then donned the overall. "What is going on?"

"You both aren't safe anymore." Mazu replied, with a sense of urgency in his voice. "We have to get you out of here."

Jay and Boro exchanged concerned looks.

"What's wrong?" Jay asked.

"I'll explain on the way," Mazu whispered. "Keep your heads low, voices even lower."

Both Jay and Boro quickly followed Mazu out of the small cubicle residence. The corridor outside was pitch dark except for a slight blue light emanating from the end of the door.

"Now, can you tell us what is going on?" Boro asked.

Mazu turned back to them, his tone very serious. "I need you to be truthful." He lowered his voice even further as he looked around surreptitiously. "How did you get here?"

"We were truthful," Jay replied back in a whisper. "I told you before, we fell through the mound, the *dambani kaur*."

"Why were you both in the desert in the first place?" Mazu asked.

"As I told you and Oran before," Jay muttered. "We were searching for ruins."

"Why?" Mazu asked with suspicion.

Jay sighed. "Because of my parents."

"Parents?" Mazu seemed interested. "What about them?"

Jay hesitated before she spoke. "They were archaeologists," Jay explained. "And they presumably died looking for the ruins of Gedrosia."

"And you came here hoping to find them? Did they know of this place?"

Jay hesitated.

76

"I need to know," Mazu ordered as they stood quietly in the corridor.

"Yes and no," Jay said finally as she opened up her backpack and took out the journal. "This belonged to my father, and it had coordinates to this place. I had no idea that this would turn out to be Gedrosia, some top-secret facility. Honestly, we were expecting some dead ruins."

Mazu grabbed the journal and scanned it, then turned to Jay with expressionless eyes. "Who else has these instructions?"

Jay gulped. "Nobody." She decided she'd better keep Erol out of this.

Mazu looked at the journal, then handed it back to Jay with intense eyes. "You are already in trouble. Your friend got away. Now come with me."

"Wait, my friend?" Jay asked urgently. "You know about him? How do you know! Is he alright?" Jay was worried for Erol. Then, she thought about the men in the black car. "Was that black car yours?"

Mazu glared at her but didn't respond. "Just follow me. Enough questions. You are in enough trouble as it is." His tone was much louder, angrier.

"Okay," Jay said quietly; Boro also shaking his head in agreement. Mazu quickly rushed outside of the main corridor. He turned around to see that Jay and Boro had not budged.

"Well? come on!" Mazu gave them a glare. "What are you both waiting for?"

"Aren't you going to holofold us?" Jay asked.

Mazu sighed. "No, just come on."

They followed Mazu through a maze of corridors, arriving at a circular walkway that went around a large atrium of a multi-storied tower.

77

"What is this?" Jay couldn't help but ask. Meanwhile, Boro had caught sight of a semi-circular deck with a low glass barrier jutting out into the atrium of the tower. Immediately, he walked up to the deck, hands on the glass barrier. Before Mazu could stop Jay, she was already rushing to catch up to Boro. They were now standing at the edge of the deck, gaping at the magnificent sight that loomed in front of them.

Staring up and down the tower's atrium length, Jay saw three floors stacked above them leading all the way up to a skylight ceiling. Below the deck were multiple floors that ran down for as long as the eye could see disappearing into darkness. Each floor was distinct in its activities though unified in style, modern with holographic displays flickering everywhere like the consoles of a spaceport control centre. Running parallel along the tower's length on opposite sides of the deck were two infinitesimally long glass elevators that connected the floors.

"What is all this?" Jay asked again, open-jawed. The view with the skylight above and the never-ending floors below was genuinely staggering.

"Quiet!" Mazu admonished. "Or else I WILL holofold you."

Jay and Boro quietly returned to Mazu's side, their faces drawn. Mazu sighed with the expression of an unhappy babysitter.

"This is the GM tower. The headquarters of this facility," Mazu replied quietly as he continued round the atrium. "And as enticing as it looks, it's not a playground. It's a top secret facility. Now come along."

The three of them continued in silence, going around the atrium until they arrived at the opposite side of the deck. They stopped in front of one of the glass elevators that ran down the building. Like clockwork, they followed Mazu into the glass elevator, starting their descent to the lower floors.

"Where are we going?" Jay said as she stared out the elevator, "You're beginning to really frighten me."

Mazu took a deep breath. "I am taking you both to a safehouse. You can leave all the questions till we are out of here."

Jay stared out at the multiple floors passing by her, her eyes focusing on the sophisticated machinery and the holographic lights that flashed everywhere. On one of the lowest floors, she saw dozens of robots working at extending a room, breaking rock, draining off the water, and filtering out weeds, or some other organics. Then, above, on one of the higher floors, she saw bots uncoiling cables, melting ducts to form insulation, and then applying insulation on wires. Still others were soldering chips. Finally, across this technical lot were the chemist bots working with beakers and test tubes, and some neon chemical. Soon enough, she had lost track of how many levels they had descended.

"Might I ask where this safehouse is?" Boro finally asked.

Before Mazu could respond, the elevator made a final stop. But the glass door did not open. Instead, a red holographic 'No Entry' sign appeared on the glass door. Mazu tapped the holographic sign and a console appeared.

"If I may have your ID, Doctor Mazu . . . thank you." A disembodied voice spoke, "Would you please put your thumbs on the plate?"

Mazu put his metal thumb on the console, the sensor scanning it until it signalled a green light. A few minutes later, the glass door automatically opened and Mazu announced, "We're here."

***

A long tunnel stretched out in front of them, extending in only one direction: straight. It was dank and poorly lit, with a single lightbulb at the far end barely lighting up the place. Metal beams lined the tunnel, just like in a mine shaft.

"Where are you taking us?" Jay asked as she exchanged a worried glance with Boro. Not oblivious to their trepidations, Mazu turned to them. "I told you before as well – you don't have to fear anything from me. We're just leaving the building."

"But this doesn't look like a normal way," Jay asked, "it looks a bit sketchy."

"It isn't the normal way, but I didn't want to deal with security." Mazu said as he crouched down to make his way through the tunnel. "Come on now."

"After you." Jay said quietly as she hunched into the tunnel after him. All three of them crawled their way to the end where a dead-end brick wall awaited them. Once a few inches away from the wall, Mazu stopped in his steps. Then, he placed his hand on one of the centre stones. It was apparently loose, so he pushed it until it sank inside.

Jay and Boro watched in curiosity, as a holographic console popped up. Mazu pressed a few numbers that led to additional prompts. After a few seconds of entering random letters and numbers, Mazu waited until the console vanished altogether.

"Mazu… what….?" Jay asked.

But Mazu held his finger up to his lips, "Just wait a minute." He pointed at the wall.

The next thing Jay saw was a luminescent blue light. Then, a holographic frame appeared, where there had once been solid stone seconds before.

Jay gasped, transfixed at the bright, blue plasma-like threads spiralling in the hologram in front of her.

Mazu grinned. "Let's go."

Before they knew it, Mazu was already walking straight into the portal-looking space, his entire body melting into the blue ember. And within seconds, all traces of the bronze-coloured android were gone.

"Where'd he go?" Jay exclaimed, then turned to Boro her mouth gaping wide. "He just vanished through that... that... portal!"

Boro meanwhile had a deadpan expression on his face. For a few minutes, he stood there in silence.

Jay tugged at him. "Boro. What's wrong? Where do you think he went?"

"Humans often say, there is only one way to find out." With that, Boro brushed past Jay, raising his right hand to the portal.

"Wait..." before Jay could stop him, Boro was gone, first his hands, then arms and finally, his entire body, all consumed in the blue ember.

Jay stared at the portal, its plasma-like surface evolving with mini-eruptions of neon light. She shuddered. *Foolish Boro, didn't even wait for me*, she thought. She looked around the tunnel one last time, sighed and then treaded slowly towards the portal. Her eyes instinctively closed in the bright luminescence, and the last thought she had was a small prayer.

Please God, let this portal not close in on me or chop my arm off.

Neither happened and instead, Jay passed through the portal safely, each step taking her closer to a new realm she would discover very soon.

***

The sight was nothing Jay could have expected. All three of them were now back at the very same place they'd met one another in—the one-roomed stone house atop the hill, with the sarcophagus and sistrum. With the air still musty, the pillars still standing on the sides, and the lantern still burning, it seemed like nothing had changed since they'd last been there.

Jay blinked a few times. "How in the world did we get *here*?"

Mazu, who seemed more relaxed once they were out of the facility, walked over to them. "Look. I'm really sorry for all this. I know you both find this confusing but we are taking a secret way out of the Compound so that no one suspects you both are gone."

Then, Mazu pointed around him, "This stone room – we call it the Grotto – is connected to the GM tower through a secret passage only a few know of. Luckily for you both, I am one of those few." Mazu waited and looked at both of them in turn to see if this all was registering. Both of them returned confused looks but since neither of them asked anything further, he signalled them both with his hands, "So, let's keep going," Mazu said as he signalled them both with his hands. "We have only a little while before I have to head back."

"What is this place?" Jay asked, excited.

"It's what Oran said – a research facility that is working to preserve living things. It was made about two decades ago when we discovered how human activities were destroying life and how vital it was to keep life going."

"So, you're one of those environmental groups?" Jay asked, confused.

Mazu rolled his eyes. "Humans and their hubris. That's what got us in this mess in the first place."

"So, why are we trying to sneak out?" Jay asked.

"And where are we going now?" added Boro.

"I will repeat again. The Compound where you were, it wasn't safe for you both." Mazu said in a serious, but gentle tone. "You both broke some very serious protocols coming here. This is a very top-secret facility. For now, I am taking you both to a safe place where you can stay until I can figure out how to send you back."

"Should we be worried?" Jay asked, though she could already feel herself filling up with dread.

"Not yet," Mazu said as he led them out of the Grotto back to the side portico. Jay stared at the magically suspended stone house and then looked up at the sunless sky, which was just as bright as they'd last seen it.

"It's not real, the sky," Mazu said as he looked up, "computer-simulated, diffused LED and plasma."

"The sky is simulated?" Jay asked, wide-eyed, "All of it?"

"All of it," Mazu said.

"What about the trees?" Jay asked. "They're real, right?"

"Yes," Mazu replied. "The trees are real—as are most other things. But there's a bit of simulation here and there to make you feel like you're 'Overground', that is the surface world."

"But why? What is the point of these simulations?" Jay asked.

"Exactly my question." Boro asked. "What is the practical purpose of this simulation when only bots seem to work here."

"Aha," Mazu finally stopped walking. "A good question." He turned to address them. "First, bots are not the only ones who work here. Humans work here as well."

"They do?" Jay sounded surprised. Not once had she encountered, seen or heard a human while she was here.

"Yes, Jay," Mazu continued. "Humans work here alongside bots. And these simulations ensure appropriate aesthetics for optimal living conditions. You see, we discovered that living creatures, humans and non-humans alike, adapted here better with an artificial sky and familiar landforms from the Overground. It is surprising for us as well to discover that aesthetics were physiologically important to living things. It might be psychosomatic but whatever the reasons, this virtual sky was essential in making this place habitable for them - humans especially."

"Interesting," Jay muttered, still staring up at the sky, "so that's all rock?"

"Yes, all rock." As Mazu said this, he led both down the colonnaded walkway that connected to the portico. They made their way down the wooded foothills which eventually led them back to the paved courtyard adjacent to the cave hill.

"That's where we landed," Jay said as she twirled around in the paved area, "we came out that cave tunnel."

"That's the Landing Dock." Mazu said. "But no one has gotten through the *dambani kaur* and the shaft, unless they had clear directions. I still don't understand how you both got here." He eyed them suspiciously. Then, he walked up to an unassuming rock on the floor. It didn't have any luminous moss like the others.

"You see this rock?" Mazu pointed at the stone with his feet. "If we move it, a vertical shaft within the cave is activated," Mazu kicked the stone and a bright blue light appeared from the cave entrance. Jay gasped.

The blue light disappeared once Mazu returned the stone back to its original position. He looked back at an incredulous Jay, continuing, "once you enter the cave, you can access a switch there that activates an electromagnetic vent. That vent will lift you directly to the *dambani kaur* in the desert."

"So why can't we return home through this shaft?" Boro asked matter-of-factly.

"You can't. You would need to be authorized to do all this. And only Oran is authorized. And from the surface, the Overground that is, you need to access the holoswitch in the desert to fall through the *dambani kaur*. How were you able to access that switch?"

"I swear, we don't know." Jay said, now worried.

"I just don't understand how you both got through." Mazu said with a heavy voice. "You both should not be here." The

84

bronze-coloured android muttered something to himself, then with a resigned sigh, motioned them to follow him.

"This part of the forest is called Pine Grove," said Mazu as he entered the forest from an unobstructed section, an underpass of overarching fir trees. Boro and Jay followed behind, noticing that the trees were perfectly lined up as if to provide a grand entrance; small sprinklers dotted the ground.

"This part of the forest is more or less planned," Mazu explained. Midway in through the underpass, Mazu stared up at the canopy of fir trees, then turned to them and spoke in a gravelly voice, "But if we go in deeper, we will enter the Ghaba. It's very different from Pine Grove. In fact, very different from any forest you've witnessed in your life. It's an underground primeval forest."

"Huh?" Jay furrowed her brows, tired of his enigmatic statements. "You mean with dinosaurs?"

But Mazu didn't respond to her question. Instead, he continued to lead them deeper in the forest.

Jay looked around, sensing that the forest around them was growing denser, darker. The trees were closer now, fighting for space and possibly even a piece of the virtual sky. All of a sudden, the entire forest seemed alive with the sound of leaves swaying and dewdrops falling. The roots were exposed, the trunks all covered with climbers and parasites. Jay stared down and noticed that even the soil underneath had begun to change. She patted Boro, and they both examined the difference: the soil had become topsoil, soft and abundant with luminous fungi, ants, and red coloured insects.

"You're right. This forest is different," Jay remarked, as she stared up in the sky. Gigantic trees with trunks thirty feet in diameter rose a hundred feet overhead. A dense canopy, that blotted out the sky, was alive with unusual sounds. Jay noticed that some of these sounds were coming from the dripping of a strange honey-coloured liquid from the tree branches. Hanging from the branches of the trunks of some of these trees were some luminous feathery leaves.

"Don't touch these leaves," Mazu cautioned her.

Despite the warning, Jay's shoulder scraped a low-hanging branch with leaves, that began to shake immediately. The tree then began to shed its leaves, releasing an unusual white powder. Jay quickly brushed the powder from her head and shoulders.

"This powder is harmless, it's pollen. But it's very valuable because these trees have limited pollen," explained Mazu. "Now that these trees have shed their pollen, they won't pollinate for another year."

"Another year?" Boro repeated. "What kind of trees are these?"

"What kind of place *is* this?" Jay added.

Mazu turned to them grinning. "I told you both before. This forest is special. And I wasn't kidding. These are ancient trees, long extinct Overground precisely for their inability to pollinate frequently." He paused and looked up at the trees. "You see, the Ghaba is an ancient subterranean forest. It already existed at the time the sanctuary was being built. And because it's underground, it has unique characteristics."

Jay stared at the trees with their knobbly trunks and exposed roots. "But is that even possible, a forest to exist underground?"

"Indeed, it is. You see, this forest dates as far back as ten thousand years ago. What we theorize is that an ancient civilization, older than even the Indus Valley civilization, cultivated crops and plants here in the underground due to the groundwater. It was eventually their cultivation that grew into this wild forest."

"And this forest has since then remained untouched?" Boro enquired as he bent down to pick a small red ant on his palm, "With all the living creatures as well?"

Mazu frowned. "No—the forest wasn't home to many of the parasites and insects you'll see. We introduced those later once we had sufficient oxygen saturation in this area. Otherwise, only animals such as moles that are well-adapted to subterranean living could have survived here."

"So, all the animals are from the surface?" Jay asked.

"Almost all of them," Mazu answered, "and it was no easy task for them to adapt to this new habitat. It took us scientists many years until we felt like this could work. A lot of effort and science has gone into ensuring that the animals and plants can live here symbiotically."

"I bet." Jay said.

"Come. I'll show you some other interesting things." Mazu gestured for them to follow him. They made their way through the forest to come to a small clearing, where large toadstool mushrooms, the size of chairs, surrounded them, growing feverishly in damp soil.

"Now, these are toadstool mushrooms that we have brought from the Overground. But as you can see, they've evolved remarkably into giant toadstools." Then, the bot patted one of the mushrooms as if it were human, "The tiniest creatures of the Earth have increased their sizes in the subterranean as their survival is not threatened. There is little competition here. In fact, some—like butterflies—have wings spanning a few yards."

"Butterflies? But how—" Jay immediately stopped talking as Mazu put a finger to his mouth, "Quiet. Listen."

They all stood still, as their ears became alert for the sound. It was a buzzing sound, that soon changed to a flapping sound. The sound grew and a swift breeze brushed over them. Jay and Boro looked up at the sight.

Mammoth butterflies, vibrantly patterned, fluttered overhead among the tree canopy, no less magnificent than tropical birds.

"This is the Monarch butterfly. Am I correct?" Boro asked, pointing at the butterfly that bore black, orange, and white patterned wings. Jay noticed that for the first time, Boro was displaying signs of a dawning curiosity, an unusual earnestness and wonder evident in his shiny, robotic eyes.

Mazu smiled at him. "It is, Boro. You're correct."

"If I am not mistaken, these butterflies went extinct a long time ago," Boro said as he examined the creatures.

"These butterflies were rescued just when they were near extinction," Mazu replied. "Now, they are preserved here in the sanctuary."

"Are they supposed to be this large?" Jay asked. "I thought butterflies were much smaller."

Mazu smiled. "You're right. Quite like those toadstool mushrooms, these Monarchs have grown much larger than the ones you'd found on the surface world. You see, with ample food and no competition—and particularly no human interference—they have grown quite large here, adapting to life underground in extraordinary ways."

"What is their original size?" Jay asked, "in the Overground that is."

"You wouldn't believe me if I told you," Mazu joked, "they are supposed to be the size of your palm."

"Oh, wow!" Jay was surprised, "that's remarkable."

"No, my dear," Mazu winked. "That's just evolution."

The three of them continued onwards, entering an overhanging tassel of moss creepers hanging down from taller fir trees. By then, Jay was convinced they had entered some otherworldly forest. This forest was no ordinary forest and Mazu had quite aptly called it special.

They continued to walk further in, until they came across a large, human-sized green nest.

"Is that a cocoon?" Boro asked, as they all came closer to it.

Mazu grinned and nodded. Jay inched closer and examined the cocoon. It was a transparent green colour. She placed her hand on it, and noticed that the cocoon had begun glowing, pulsing, and the shape inside was moving now, slowly at first and then vigorously.

"Step aside," Mazu ordered them. All of them stepped back, waiting timorously behind the cocoon until the creature inside broke through its shell, emerging into the light. Soon, its wings swelled up, growing firmer, until it flew away past them. It was a large moth.

"This is quite extraordinary," Jay remarked. "A world without humans has allowed these moths and butterflies to thrive incredibly."

Meanwhile, Boro walked over to the cocoon, touching the broken shell. "Mazu, how much of this is natural?" he asked.

"What do you mean?"

"What I am trying to ask is, how many of the processes going on here such as the metamorphosis are naturally occurring, and how many of these processes are controlled by you?"

"They're all natural, Boro. However, this is a research laboratory like any other," Mazu informed him. "It's still a controlled environment. That part is still unnatural."

"And do you happen to conduct experiments on them?" Boro asked.

"Sometimes," Mazu nodded in a manner to suggest this was nothing out of the ordinary.

Jay was perturbed by the revelation. "But I thought this was a sanctuary for animals, not a place to conduct experiments on them. Isn't that unethical?"

"Jay, we aren't doing any unethical research here," Mazu sounded defensive. "We are doing research that will ensure that these species are preserved. That they continue to flourish for years to come."

"What kind of research are you exactly conducting here?" Boro enquired.

"Well, for the most part, we are merely observers, studying the subterranean ecosystems here in Gedrosia, how animals and plants interact and what factors lead to a net increase in biodiversity."

"And will these animals be eventually freed into the wild?" Jay folded her arms.

"Look, Jay," Mazu leaned forward, "this research is critical to ensure the survival of human beings. It's critical for our survival. Without this research, humans beings are at the brink of extinction."

Jay looked up at him, colour draining from her face. "What are you talking about?"

Mazu narrowed his eyes, his voice ominous. "I don't think people in the Overground—your world—understand the severity of the HumanX Project and the implications of our past actions," He lowered his voice, as Jay came closer, "The human species is very much going to go extinct Jay, unless –"

"Unless what?" she asked anxiously.

"Unless these sanctuaries figure out a way to ensure that biological diversity is kept intact."

CHAPTER 11

Res Complex

Jay and Boro continued to follow Mazu, a profound silence lingering among them. The excitement Jay felt earlier was replaced by a strange sense of dread. If what he had told them was true, then humans were truly headed for their own demise. And the unfortunate part was that most of them were oblivious to this fact.

"So, how much longer to the safehouse?" Jay asked, trying to finally break the silence.

"Not too long. Come along." Mazu pointed up ahead at the radiant gleams of light that shone through the tree trunks. All three paced towards the opening. They emerged from the forest into a wide open plain. The land was flat and desolate, with no vegetation.

"It almost feels like we are back in the Makran desert," Jay suggested, then turned to Mazu. "Are we back Overground?"

"No," Mazu chuckled. "We're still underground. This place is another part of Gedrosia. But since it has fewer water channels and no underground water shafts, it happens to be very dry."

Mazu signalled them to keep up as they followed him through the opening. He quickly took a left turn, skirting the forest edge and arriving at a grassy patch. There, behind a hedge of unusually small trees were two vehicles; they were four-seater pods, held by hydraulic wheels with a small hook winch at the back. Jay had only ever seen such pods at mines and excavation sites in the Maka province where they were used for dragging carts containing ores.

"Our journey hereon will be on these." Mazu jumped into one of the pods, tapping his badgecard on one of the side scanners on the pod, bringing it to life. "These are Landstorm pods. They are powered by hydrogen."

Boro and Jay joined Mazu in the pod which turned on silently. The three commenced their drive through the rough prairie terrain, which felt unusually slick. It was as if they were hovering over it.

"The wheels are made from plasma fibre which allows them to glide and hover over the rocks, moulding into the form of whichever terrain they're on," Mazu explained, noticing Jay's curiosity. "Plus, they are extremely light."

They continued their smooth ride through the dry plain. Far ahead, a dull brown mass loomed along the horizon. Around it, the plain stretched away into the barren grey-coloured hills which shut off their view at a distance of a few miles.

"So, where is this safehouse that you speak off?" Boro asked as he stared out hypnotically through the window.

"You're going to find out soon enough," Mazu replied, and then revved the pod, placing full power on its forward thrusters. The pod gained momentum and in some fifteen minutes, they had gone through the empty desert terrain. Finally, a gravel road came into view. Mazu slowed down, pulling into it and continuing some hundred meters along the road.

The area suddenly became darker, as if a switch had been turned off.

"This is the first stage of nightfall," Mazu explained. "The skylight simulates the normal progression of the day."

After continuing along the road, the pod stopped. They had arrived at an elevated deck that looked out over a wide valley below.

The valley was dark. To the far left, one could see radial rows of tiny flickering lights visible, arranged around a dark space with a reflection, most likely some body of water. This section was separated from a large compound by a boundary wall and an overpass.

The compound was massive, a fleet of metal hulks standing at one corner, and neatly stacked rows of modular containers and warehouses stood on the other. It was surrounded by a mesh boundary wall, expect where it connected to the overpass. At the centre of this massive complex was a large tower, a colossal skeleton of steel and iron, rising from limbs of unequal length embedded in the ground. A single upright beam reached up some fifty feet into the sky, dwarfing everything around them.

"That is the Main Compound, which we just left." Mazu explained as he pointed ahead.

Jay looked confused. "We took such a roundabout way to get out of there. Couldn't we have gone through that overpass tunnel?"

"We took a *safer*, albeit complicated route. You see those bots," Mazu pointed to the oversized, armoured bots wearing uniform that flanked the boundary wall. "Those are servitor bots, known as Jotuns," Mazu pointed at them. "They would not have allowed you to leave."

"What would they do to us if they saw us leave?" Boro asked.

"Nothing good, I am afraid." Mazu said solemnly.

"I see." Jay gulped.

Mazu returned his attention to the Compound and then pointed at a large sprawling building with the tower standing over it. "See there?" Mazu said as he pointed to the tower, "that's the Control tower, the GM tower, where we operate the physical structure of Gedrosia, the sky, the hills, the day, the night… it's all simulated. And that pole above the tower is what projects the cloudless sky." A pause, and then he looked over his shoulder, back at Jay, "You can't have a sky under the ground now, can you?"

"Yes, well, right," Jay said as she looked back at the tower, watching it fade into the illusion of the sky, merging with and supporting the ceiling of this huge, underground cavern. "It's quite incredible."

"Indeed. Technology and AI can take us quite far," Mazu sounded contemplative, "if we allow them to, that is. Fear will only hold us back."

Jay wondered whether Mazu was making a reference to what was happening to bots all over the world. Indeed, he was not wrong; the Overground world had regressed in some ways because of its fear of bots.

Within the Compound, Jay could also see tens of pods lined up single file, driving towards the overpass, which provided an opening in the mesh border that surrounded the Compound. It appeared to be gated on one end, but with no Jotun guarding it. Instead, a single tower overhead performed some form of identity scan. Further past the gates, a driveway was visible lined along both sides by a mesh gate and poles that stood like sentinels along the way.

"Where are all these pods going?" Jay asked Mazu.

"Where we are also going. To the Res Complex where the humans live," Mazu said.

"How many humans live here?" Boro asked.

"Around two hundred; the rest are bots."

"And what are those buildings?" Boro asked, as he pointed at the buildings at the periphery of the boundary wall.

"Just some older buildings," Mazu said. "They're part of an abandoned compound."

Surrounding the complex, quite a distance away were rows upon rows of unusual hills that faded into mist.

"And might I ask if those hills at the fringes form the outer extents of Gedrosia?" Boro enquired as he stared out into the distance.

"Yes, yes," Mazu said, almost sounding annoyed. "Now can we take a break from some questions please?"

Jay and Boro smiled and nodded.

Mazu finally started the descent from the elevation, taking a small gravel road that became a driveway leading into the valley. Soon, a network of converging roads came into view, and the lights transformed into two-story homes. Further away, other lights were visible, perhaps more scattered townhomes, and then even further, in the distance were the dark shadows of the hills and mist.

All the two-story homes looked identical in the dusky darkness, each house with a hedge around it and a low gate with a holosign. The holosigns had an identifying number which transformed into a name as the pod drove past them. Sometimes, the gates were open, and one could catch a glimpse of green patches at the front. Driving past the homes, Jay took note of the different numbers and names that appeared. Finally, the pod slowed down in front of number 21.

"That's you." Mazu pointed at a purple neon light sign, its number shifting into "R&D." He pulled over beside the gate and disembarked, the others following him. Past the small wooden gate, they walked along a stone pathway through the garden, leading them to the entrance door.

Mazu knocked on the door and turned to Jay. "Welcome to your home for a few days. You'll be safe here."

CHAPTER 12

Safehouse

The door was opened by a short man with dark hair and large, beady eyes. His small grey beard stood out from his face, long and unruly. He didn't come across as the typical scientist given his attire; the white shirt underneath and a brown waistcoat on top. The silver buttons on the waistcoat stood out, as did his black shoes which had slightly pointy toes.

"Mazu? At your service!" the man bowed in front of the bot. "What can I do for you?"

"Raul, this is Jay and Boro," Mazu introduced them. "They're from the Overground."

"Overground?" Raul repeated after a moment of silence.

Mazu kept going. "I'd be grateful if you can keep them here, safe. I have to head back to the Main Compound and sort out paperwork so that they can get home quickly." Without waiting for any response, Mazu looked at Jay and gave her what seemed to be a very robotic quick hug. "Take care child." After that, Mazu dashed into his pod and drove off without leaving any time for Raul to lodge any dissent.

They were all still in the doorway with their mouths open in shock. Raul shook his head as if trying to come off a daze and turned to Jay and her bot. "Well then! I guess that's that! Why don't you both come on inside and make yourselves at home? I'll introduce you to my wife, Delara." Jay gave him a hesitant look but followed him inside his home after he offered a graceful smile.

The entrance was a snug circular room with two small passageways and a staircase. They went through one of the passages and arrived in a decorative living area, reminiscent of Kolachi homes. The room was cluttered, with antique wood furniture, fluffy couches, oriental carpets hanging on the wall, as well as alternatives images of an oriental city and calligraphy floating around.

Raul took a seat on one of the old armchairs and motioned to one of the couches. "Well go on, child. Sit. I won't bite."

Jay nodded and took a seat on one of the couches, its plushness suggesting it was hardly ever used. Boro stood beside the couch, eyeing the home surreptitiously.

Meanwhile, a matronly lady came out to the room, her eyes wide open, possibly in surprise or shock. She reminded Jay of one of her schoolteachers, with her long-braided hair and open-toed sandals. The lady stared at Raul, narrowing her eyes, then took a seat on a chair beside Jay and Boro. She finally turned to Jay, her eyes warm but disciplined.

"I'm Delara, Raul's wife." The lady said.

"Jay, and this is Boro. Thank you for letting us stay with you." Jay said awkwardly. "I don't know what's going on, but Mazu told us to stay here until they figure out how to get us back home."

"Well, I'm sure he will figure it out!" Raul said uncomfortably. "What are you both doing here in the first place?"

Jay let out a laugh. "It's a long story."

"It must be." Delara nodded. "This is a top-secret facility."

Jay noticed the sarcasm. She gulped. "You see it's actually really funny..." She looked at them and neither one seemed amused.

Boro cleared his throat. "Jahan and myself were simply searching for ancient ruins given our interest in archaeology."

Jay shook her head and continued, "This was just meant to be a short trip - fun adventure for someone from Kolachi." The more Jay spoke, the more she realized how ridiculous she sounded.

Raul raised his eyebrows. "On your own? In the Makran?"

"For an *adventure*?" Delara added.

Jay felt embarrassed. "Honestly, we had no idea we would end up in this much trouble. I mean, from Pasni, one thing led to another, and we fell through one of the mud mounds – the *dambani kaur* I believe they're called," Jay took a deep breath, "so that's how we came here."

Raul frowned. "But how did you find the *dambani kaur* in the first place? And how did you get in through it? You can't just fall through the mounds unless you knew the exact location of this place or have been here before…" Raul eyed her suspiciously.

"None of us knew that this place even existed!" Boro said in an unusually loud voice for a bot. He took it a few notches down. "Look. It really is as Jay says it is. We fell through one of the mounds. That's all," Then he added, "I imagine there might be a problem with the security here. The facility is not as top secret as it seems."

Delara coughed uncomfortably. "Well, enough of this. Tell me Jay, you said you are from Kolachi?" The lady had quickly changed the subject as Raul shrank back in his seat in frustrated confusion.

Jay shook her head. "Yes, indeed."

"Oh my goodness! We haven't been there for…." Delara paused, then her expression became sad. "Maybe twenty years?"

"Will you be going there any time soon?" Jay asked.

Delara gave a polite smile. "Not sure how soon. Mazu will let us know when."

"So, you both can't leave this place just like that?" Jay asked.

Raul and Delara exchanged glances. "Not so easily." Raul continued, "If we leave, we can't ever return. This is really a top-secret facility, so we plan to leave once we are done with our work and ready."

"And right now, we have important work to do here." Delara added. "The future of humanity depends on it."

Jay sensed that something was off, and Raul and Delara were probably not telling her the entire truth.

In the meantime, Delara excused herself, her face definitely more downtrodden. When she left the room, Raul turned to Jay, this time his expressions forlorn. "Jay, we were recruited by some of the older management here. At that time, we didn't know what was going on. We didn't know."

Boro asked. "What do you mean?"

"What didn't you know?" Jay asked, confused.

Raul looked nervous, his forehead now creasing with multiple lines. "Too many secrets. Too many. You both must be confused... worried even, but for your own good, don't ask too many questions." His words carried sinister overtones, "It might get you in trouble." Jay was curious, but she didn't prod on, knowing full well that she might make her host uncomfortable again. "I understand," she said, as she gulped. In the meantime, Delara interrupted them, an interjection that was quite welcome. "Dinner's ready!"

***

There was chicken, rice and an assortment of curries and salads. Jay hadn't seen such fresh food for a long while, but she'd lost all her appetite after Raul's ominous words. Why would she get in any more trouble than she was already in? Was their crime so grave? She looked at Boro who remained unusually quiet as well.

"Jay, are you okay?" Delara asked. "You look frightfully pale."

"Oh, it's nothing," Jay waved her hand dismissively, "I'm just a little hungry, that's all." She wasn't lying, her stomach had been rumbling for a while. "Right Boro?"

Boro shook his head. "Yes, this human has been without food for quite a long time!"

Quickly, Jay took a bite of the food and felt better. "It's delicious!" Jay piled her plate with more food, and much to her relief, the lingering fears had somewhat dissipated. In fact, by the end of the meal, she was feeling content and sleepy.

"You must have been famished," Delara remarked, "now you have some colour in your cheeks!"

Jay stared at her stomach, bloated from the food. "You're right. All I can think about now is sleeping."

"Well, I can show you to your room upstairs if you want." Delara offered. "And I'll leave water and tea on the kitchen counter if you need it." Delara turned to Boro. "Can you give me a hand? " The bot nodded.

Jay retired to the guest room given to her – a room in the attic, with a small floor mat. She kicked off her shoes, sprawling face-down on the floor, as a wave of fatigue rolled over her. Rolling over, she propped up her head with the pillow and reviewed the situation. It seemed like there was much to figure out yet, but there was a great discovery that had already been made. She wasn't crazy. There is such a place as Gedrosia, she thought. But she and Boro were not supposed to be here. She wondered how long it would take for Mazu to come and get them. Then, her thoughts returned to Raul's warning. What did he mean?

Jay tried to brush it off, but there was something unsettling about her hosts. She tried to distract herself, and then wondered where Boro was and when he would come upstairs. Finally, she heard the bot talking with Delara and the sound of dishes being washed. She sighed, then left the door open for him to come, as she dozed off into a fatigued slumber.

***

That night, Jay dreamt again about her parents. It was the same dream she had had in the desert, where they were conducting excavations. The dream would then end in an earthquake.

But this time, she saw more. She saw her parents speaking to a man she recognized. She concentrated hard. It was Uncle Salim. The professor looked younger, with darker, fuller hair. Jay's parents were standing beside him, talking to him. They looked concerned, trying to warn him of some impending danger. *What was the danger?* Then all three of them turned to stare down at someone.... It was Jay herself, standing at the excavation site. *How could I be there? Jay thought.* Suddenly, she wasn't sure if this was a dream, a memory or a figment of her imagination.

Jay's dreams took her back to Kolachi. She seemed to be on a deserted beach, simple and barren, with a light tower visible from afar. Light drizzle fell from a cold grey sky, mingling with the spray from a grey sea. The scene was hardly inspiring, though there was a tinge of familiarity and warmth. She and her mother were collecting shells, while her father was returning from a small ramshackle store, with cups of warm tea in his hands.

Okay, Jay thought. She was obviously making this up in her head. She had never remembered her parents so well, nor did she remember the beach. How was this possible? Then, as she went back to her dream.

The beach was gone, but now she was back in her childhood home. She remembered it well. It was the place where her family had lived for several years and where she was born. The dream took her to her favourite rooms, including the attic which housed the library. It had been a refuge from the world, not to mention a source of the one thing that kept her excited, day to day.

Jay woke up and switched on her bedside light and sat there, thinking of what she had just seen. How could she remember all these things as such a young child? She got up and went into the outdoor lounge. Everyone was asleep and Boro was powered down, sitting on the chaise in the lounge. She tiptoed to the common pantry outside and picked up a cup, filling it with hot water from the dispenser. Then she dumped a teabag, milk and sugar into the cup. *Tea will calm me down*. After she had a warm cup of tea, she went back to her room, half-dazed and tired, as she curled up in her bed.

This time though, instead of her dreams, she could hear the murmur of a conversation taking place in the room downstairs. In her daze, she could make out bits and pieces of what was spoken, though nothing that she could make sense of.

She tried to let it all go, trying to fall back into sleep, but instead was left in a dazed state once more, until finally when everything was silent, she fell into a deep and dreamless sleep, the first of many.

✱ ✱ ✱

"You need to be careful of what you tell the girl," Jay heard Delara say.

"It doesn't matter," Raul said. "Nothing matters."

"Why are you saying this?"

"Because we *are* doomed. Photosynthesis is down eighty per cent," said Raul. "I just took some readings today. Many species are missing, and others can't survive! Subterranean sunlight is also impacting photosynthesis."

"And how many scientists have confirmed this?"

"We all know, Delara. The Syndicate isn't interested in saving humanity; it is spending its money elsewhere. We know that the Sanctuaries are just a cover up!"

"We don't have proof."

"And we may never have proof." Raul sounded hopeless. "What's the good of anything? I don't see—"

"You don't need to see!" said Delara. "We only have two options. Either we think about leaving, or we continue this lie. Either way, we lose our lives. It's the future we want to save."

"Then, let's leave." Raul said. "Let's go home to the Overground."

"To the Overground." Delara repeated.

CHAPTER 13

Dystopia

The room was still dark, only a hint of dawn light filtering in through the tiny windows in the attic. Jay reached in the dark, her hand brushing against an object. It was a tiny clock on the table next to her. She stared at it in confusion. It said 5 AM. Was it there before? She stared at it in confusion. Was it there before? She looked around. The room appeared to be a little different from what she remembered it. Then, she heard another sound, a rustling of bedsheets and a shadow. Someone was in the room with her. She yelled out loud, only to finally wake up. There was no clock beside her and no window.

Oh, just a dream, Jay thought to herself. *Can't I even get a night's sleep without something weird happening to me.*

She drifted back to sleep only to awake a few hours later from the sound of breaking glass. Her eyes opened and for a few moments, she lay there on the bed, staring blankly at the ceiling. She wondered if she was still dreaming as the events from the past two days unravelled in her head: Mazu and Oran, the primeval forest, the strange sky – and yesterday's rushed exit from the Compound. This was no dream, she was certain of that. This was Gedrosia and she was in the home of a couple, Raul and Delara. She tried to recall the garbled conversation she overheard last night, trying to decipher what they meant by the photosynthesis? She wasn't sure if *that* was a dream.

After a bit of bewildered thinking, Jay scrambled out of the bed. Quickly, she tidied her dishevelled hair with her hands, ready to go downstairs to greet her hosts. She walked out of the room, her pace slower as she climbed down the stairs. It was oddly quiet. By the time she was in the lounge, she knew something was wrong.

The room was in complete disarray. Papers were strewn all over the floor, and the tube was switched on, muted. But Raul and Delara were nowhere in sight. Boro was sitting on the chaise in the lounge still powered off, his head hanging lifelessly. Jay walked over to him, turning on the switch on his neck, waiting for him to restart. Then, she marched into the dining room and saw that the table was laid out with crockery for three people. At the centre was an untouched breakfast of orange juice and toast. Still, no sign of people. Something didn't seem right. She thought back to yesterday and wondered what Raul and Delara were talking about. They had said something about leaving for the Overground. What if they had left?

Jay scanned the dining area and noticed a broken teacup next to the kitchen counter. Was there a fight? She walked over to the counter and sniffed. There was a faint smell of something awful coming from the kitchen area. After uncovering some disgusting cobwebs and dust, she found that the source of the stench was molded cheese. She quivered with disgust at the sight. Then, she quickly glanced over at Boro, now activated. She ran to him.

"Boro, have you seen Raul and Delara?"

The bot shrugged. "I am afraid not. I have been switched off for the past nine hours."

By then, Jay was running around in the lounge, calling out for Raul and Delara. She returned to the lounge dejected.

"I don't suppose you heard their conversation last night?"

"Like I said, I have no knowledge of what transpired since yesterday."

Jay looked at the bot, worry in her eyes. "Well, I overheard them, and it sounded like they were leaving Gedrosia."

Boro leaned forward. "Are you sure it was not one of your dreams?"

"Of course not!" Jay got up, her face red, as she started pacing. Truth be told, she wasn't sure herself. She could have easily dreamt this up, but her gut feeling was that it was real. Then, she finally sank back in the chair. "I actually *wish* it was a dream, because whatever they were discussing didn't sound like it was something good."

"We can simply wait for them. They will return." Boro seemed unperturbed, as he got up and opened the kitchen cupboard to scavenge for some food. "They must have left to run errands." The bot then handed out some bars to Jay that he found in the cupboard. "And look what I have found! This looks like chocolate!"

Jay frowned, then pushed away the bars being offered to her. "Boro, look around! This place looks like a mess. Something has happened to them."

"Is this an unusual level of 'mess' for humans? I find humans to be quite 'messy' as a matter of course."

"Obviously it is! Or else, I won't be so concerned."

Boro looked at the table. "It does seem somewhat illogical to prepare a meal and then leave without eating it."

Jay was about to pull her hair. She pointed at the floor. "And the floor! Look at it, its covered in papers!"

"An unusual, though not unique degree of chaos for a human habitation." The bot agreed.

"Urgh." Jay stomped her feet. "We seriously need to get you some upgrades. How are you unable to see that something went wrong here? Why are you being like this?"

She continued to give the bot a glaring look, until finally Boro nodded. "Alright, fine! I suppose you are right to assume that something might have happened. But I do not think that we should jump to conclusions. I still think the best course of action is to stay put here until they return. I trust these humans over the bots here."

Jay frowned. "We need to get out of here."

"I was afraid you would say that." Boro sounded miserable. "I would prefer that we stay here. We will be safe here at least."

"Well, I think you're wrong!" she asserted. "No one, not even Mazu, is coming for us! And now that Raul and Delara have gone, I am not waiting around for anyone's permission."

Boro stared at her unwavering eyes. "Fine. And how do you expect us to find a way out?"

"I think I have an idea."

***

Outside, the Gedrosian world was glorious, the skylight bestowing it a strange vibrancy. Unlike the dark valley they had seen the night before, this world appeared animated, a vision from old holos that Jay used to watch as a kid. The sky, the garden and the stone path leading up to the fence appeared in high-definition, with saturated hues and lights emptied of glare. Perhaps this was how a place looked like when lit up by an artificial light source. Jay didn't know the answer, but what she did know was that Gedrosia in the day looked certainly very different from what it looked during the night.

"The hedge gate is open," Boro pointed as he ran out the gate to inspect the area outside.

"What is it?" Jay asked as she watched him bob his metal head around.

"It seems that the pod is also missing." Boro blocked the gate entrance, as he folded his arms. "They have gone somewhere."

Jay frowned. "Right. Why would they make all that mess before they left?"

"I don't know but I still don't think it is wise for us to be loitering around in a place where we aren't supposed to be in the first place."

"Maybe, but I'd rather take that chance and try to find a way out myself. Besides, Erol must be worried sick."

She gave the bot a decisive look, then pushed past him, walking out the gate and down the road. Boro threw his arms up in defeat and followed along, conducting their journey in silence. They marched along the driveway, walking past the rows of identical homes, all standing silently like cardboard boxes. Far ahead, they saw the complex surrounded by an empty expanse of grey bedded stone that eventually ended in a hill barrier. Within the barrier, Jay saw the overpass and what was unmistakably an open tunnel.

"That's it!" Jay pointed at the dark hollow that was visible in the rock barrier, "The tunnel should lead us to the Compound!"

"But remember what Mazu said." Boro eyed it suspiciously from afar. "We shouldn't be roaming around here."

"Well, let's go towards it and see if we can get through without getting seen by any bots. We might even see someone who could help us."

"Fine!" Boro said. "But we only talk to humans. I don't trust the bots here."

Both of them continued along the road that seemed to ascent and lead to the hill barrier. The ascent was steeper than Jay imagined, and she signalled for a rest. Somewhere in the middle of their ascent, they sat down and looked down at the valley below them.

It was a shallow bowl surrounded by grey-brown hills, all cliff-like in appearance that vanished into the sky, forming a single line boundary. A thin layer of cloudy mass blurred the sky-hill boundary. The houses in the complex appeared as shiny specks reflecting the skylight. Around them, the land leading up to the hills was grey and flat, a patchwork of stone and green. The entire area was bedded with small sections of limestone pavement. Interspersed between these small stone beds was green fern and moss growing wildly.

"Karst," Boro remarked.

"Huh?" Jay looked at him funny.

"That is what you call this landscape."

Jay nodded, then continued looking pensively at the valley. It was oddly silent. There was no movement, not even wind.

"Where is everyone?"

"Another question that remains on the unanswered list. I wish I know what to say."

After their brief rest, Boro and Jay continued along the road, finally reaching the apex. Up ahead, the tunnel was in clear sight. It was bored into a large stone hill overpass, that was a darker hue than the other hills in the area. They walked further up to the tunnel, and peeped into it. It was pitch black, the other side not in sight.

Jay hesitated, "What if it doesn't open up on the other side?" She turned to Boro, worry in her eyes. "Boro, can you check it out?"

Boro nodded, flashing his eyelights as he took the lead, treading very carefully into the tunnel. They walked slowly along the edge, their hands out, and their eyes and ears alert for any change.

"Look ahead," Boro said, pointing in front, "there is an opening."

Sure enough, Jay could make out a sliver of light. Both of them hurried forward in the direction of the opening, finally emerging from the tunnel visibly relieved to see daylight again.

"Are we maybe Overground?" Jay asked, hoping that perhaps they had actually walked up to the surface.

"I'm afraid not." Boro said as he pointed ahead.

Up ahead, they saw some steel sheds and random buildings scattered about. These sheds appeared to be out of use, their paint chipped, with moss growing all over them. A little further away, several other buildings came into view, some as high as three stories.

"It looks empty," Jay said as she walked into the small compound. Something about these buildings was eerie. All of them looked old and rusty, appearing empty at least from the windows. In fact, there was no movement in this compound either, no pods or bots as far as the eye could see. A little further was a taller concrete tower, its pinnacle concealed by the clouds. It looked almost identical to the one in the GM tower building.

Closer now, they could see that the buildings were in disrepair, overgrown with foliage and material chipping off from all odds and ends.

"I think we should go back," Boro said, looking rather uneasy. "This place is completely abandoned."

"It won't take more than..." before Jay could finish her sentence, she heard the sound of metal clinking. Jerking and turning around, she found herself staring down at a large, decapitated android, half buried in the sand. One leg was torn off, frayed wires emerging from it, but his head and arms were intact, attached to his torso.

"Sorry!" she squeaked with horror as she'd almost walked over it. The bot didn't respond. He stared at Jay first, then at Boro, his green eyes flickering in the grey light. They stared back, unsure of how to respond. Finally, the bot's eyes took on a red shade as his

110

body began to shake furiously. The bot lifted his arm to reach out to Jay. Jay reached out as well. In that instant, the bot grabbed her by the arm, pressing it hard. Jay shrieked in pain and tried to jerk back but to no avail. The droid's grip was strong, and he only pressed harder. In that instant, Boro came back from behind, holding a large metal rod in his hand which he hammered onto the bot's neck. Immediately, the bot let go of Jay's arm, who at once lost balance, falling to the ground. As she got up, she felt something heavy on her one of her feet. She looked down and saw the bot's severed metal arm still clinging to her ankle. Boro thrust at the bot's metal arm, many times over. Then, he scraped it away from Jay's foot. As the arm fell off, Jay stared in shock, first at the blotch of blood on her ankle, then at the arm writhing and pulsating on the ground. She didn't linger on any longer in this place. Quickly, she grabbed Boro's hand as he helped her up, and both ran back in the direction of the tunnel, away from this complex of horrors, at top speed.

✳ ✳ ✳

Jay and Boro took some relief inside the tunnel, realizing that no one was chasing them.

"Are you alright?" Boro asked as he stopped to examine her wounded ankle with his eyelights.

"I think so," Jay said as she bent down to check on her ankle, which had stopped bleeding. "What *was* that thing?"

"A crazy bot," Boro said as he tore a piece of her tattered jeans and wound it around the wound on her ankle. "How does it feel now?"

"Better," Jay muttered as they continued into the tunnel, back where they had come from.

Some steps in, they saw the opening. But they also saw something else.

"I think I see some shadow." Jay said. Slowly, they inched towards the opening but stopped when they saw what was in front. Up ahead was an armoured bot- the Jotun—resting his legs on one of the large boulders that seemed to be sitting next to the tunnel. Jay and Boro exchanged a quick glance.

Both of them were about to turn back but stopped when they heard one of the Jotuns call out to them.

"Hey stop, both of you! Come here."

Jay and Boro complied and walked outside to the tunnel where the Jotun inspected them. Then, he pressed the gadget around his ear and within seconds, two other armoured Jotuns emerged from the sides of the tunnel.

"What's your name?" one of the Jotuns asked Jay, as he held up an arm blocking Boro.

"Jahan," she spoke with as much calmness as she could muster, "Jahan Jumander. Is everything okay?"

"Jahan Jumander, what are you doing roaming around here. You should be at the Compound. How did you both get out?"

"I ... was just exploring-" Jay managed to only stutter, knowing that she could not reveal how they had left the Compound.

The Jotun grabbed her arm. "Come with me. You and your bot are under arrest."

"Arrest! For what?" Jay tugged at her arm but the Jotun only grasped it tighter.

"Gentlemen, can we please speak to Mazu or Oran," Boro said in his most diplomatic tone. "They can explain everything!"

The Jotuns didn't budge, and Jay continued to struggle, then stared at Boro hoping he'd be able to help. But Boro seemed equally lost on what to do. He wasn't a combat bot.

"Let me go!" but Jay's pleas were useless. She was desperate, a rush of angry emotions filled up inside her. Suddenly, she felt a metal hand on her shoulder, followed by a tiny prick. It was one of the Jotuns. She stared at him confused, then felt a rush of chemicals enter her body. Immediately, her body went limp. By then, everything was out of her control, and she was struggling to stand on her feet.

"Boro..." her voice trailed off as she fell to the ground, consciously watching everything unfold. The last thing she remembered was Boro somehow appearing out of the shadows, pushing the surprised Jotun aside and giving him a hard knock on his neck, incapacitating him. She fell to the ground, watching everything around her move in slow motion. The other two Jotuns had drawn their weapons but Boro held on to the injured one, using his body as a shield while he averted their beams. Through blurry eyes, she watched him smack them hard, and what followed was a brawl between Boro and the three Jotuns as her delirium took over. Her head was still spinning as the image of the armoured Jotuns fighting, flickered around her. Arms grabbed at Boro but he managed to break free, but this was the last image she remembered as she fell into a deep sleep.

When Jay regained consciousness, she was startled, but unable to move. A pounding headache gripped her, and her entire body felt sore. Still lying on the ground, she turned her head to see Boro lying motionless beside her, his arm dislocated, wires springing out from every suture. She still felt dazed but was able to make out the shadow of a man from the farther end of the tunnel running towards them. She closed her eyes and prayed for hope.

CHAPTER 14

Azlan's Chambers

The first thing Jay saw when she woke up was a vintage lamp with fleur-de-lis. She blinked a few times certain she was in someone else's home. Groaning, she rolled on to the other side to inspect her surroundings. She was in a minimally furnished room, likely a makeshift room, in some underground bunker of sorts. The walls and ceilings were all damp and smooth stone. Other than her own bed, the only other piece of furniture was a chair and shelf combo at the far-right corner.

Jay had no idea where she was or how she got there. She tried to recall the fight with the bots. *Yes, it was obvious they were trying to kill her. But why? Was her offence that grave? Maybe, Boro was right all along about these bots. Something was strange about them. Where was Boro? Was he alright?* Jay panicked, realizing what a terrible mistake she had made coming here.

Still in bed, she was alerted to the sound of loud thuds. Frightened, she half-closed her eyes pretending to be asleep. From the fringes, she watched a man enter the room, grab a book from the shelf and take a seat on the wooden chair. The man was probably in his fifties, though in excellent form. He was muscular and tanned despite living underground. His long brown hair hung loosely around his shoulders, and his chin was unshaved, revealing a dark grey stubble.

Who was this man and what did he want with her? Instantly, something inside Jay tightened, and she felt a strange sense of panic. She needed to escape from this place. No one could be trusted here, neither the bots, nor the humans. The thoughts only made the aches in her body worse, as she tried to shovel up her feelings and hold back her tears.

Meanwhile, the man, fully absorbed in reading his book was paying no heed to her. *Good*, she thought. *Maybe, when he leaves the room, I'll try to figure out how to escape.* But where was she?

"Where am I?" Jay realized her voice wasn't audible. In fact, the stranger barely heard her. She took a deep breath, and then mustered the courage to repeat the question loudly.

"Where am I?" It was hardly more than a whimper.

The stranger looked at her, then returned to his book. When he seemed to have reached a convenient point to stop, he put it down and looked again at Jay. "You're in my home within the Makran tunnels. And you're safe, Jahan Jumander."

"Wait, how do you know my name?" Jay tried to stay calm but could feel her heart beating louder. "Who are you?"

"Calm down, child," the man said in a low voice. "The name's Azlan, and fo' your information, you murmured your name when I carried you here. Do you remember anythin'?"

Jay frowned, doubt beginning to assail her. Was he telling the truth? Was she really safe? She tried hard to remember what had happened. There was a man who had come running to her when the Jotuns attacked her, a man who carried her through some dark tunnels. Was it this man who rescued her? She didn't know for sure, so she dared not trust him. She dared not trust anyone.

In fact, all Jay wanted to do was to find Boro and get out of here as fast as she could. But first, she needed to figure out how to get out of these tunnels. Slowly, the girl tested her strength and tried to sit up. Azlan was paying no attention – he remained fully engaged in the book. *Great*, Jay thought. *Now all I need to do is distract and dash!*

"What is it that you're reading?" Jay asked.

Azlan smiled as he took off his glasses and placed them on the table next to him. "Studyin' these ancient tunnels of Gedrosia. Suppose they might come in handy when one needs to escape…"

Jay raised her eyebrows. *Why would this man want to escape? In any case, this book could help her too.* In fact, she decided that while she's escaping, she'll try to take it too. The question was, how?

"I saw your fight with those guards," Azlan said as he finally closed the book and got up to walk over to the shelf. "I thought you were a goner. They'd have killed you, you know. Those Jotuns have no mercy."

"I suppose I have you to thank," Jay muttered, but remained guarded in her words.

Azlan frowned. "Maybe. But more your bot. He's loyal, that one. Deflected the attack. Even though he fought his own."

Then, Azlan dragged his chair to the bedside. "What did they want from you?"

"I don't know," Jay was in no mood to tell this man, a stranger no less, anything about herself. She folded her arms across her chest, "Where's my bot? Is he alright?" she asked.

Azlan pointed at the edge of the bed. Jay lifted herself and beside the ledge, saw Boro's body lying there lifeless. There were two visible burn marks on his chest plate and a large dent on his head. Jay gasped.

"Don't worry, he'll be okay," Azlan made a dismissive gesture with his hand. "His injuries are superficial. The problem's with his neural network. I've had to format him."

"What? You did *what*?!" Jay jerked and got up.

"Don't worry, I made sure his memories are intact and he's the same person…I mean bot," Azlan reassured her. "Just needed to remove some data leading up to the fight with the Jotuns."

Jay raised her brows. "Why'd you need to remove those?"

"Cuz' he needs to forget he fought his own: bots. Messes up their consciousness…" Azlan looked a bit sad.

Jay raised one brow, an incredulous expression on her face, "Bot consciousness?"

"It's not consciousness the way you or I see it. It's neural networks. See, bots are connected through data networks. They do have some sense of self-actualization. That's why it took him a while to offer you help."

Before Jay could seek more explanation, she was caught off guard by a sharp pain reverberating through her head.

"What?... My head … oww."

"Orite. Hold still. Can't have you talkin' in this condition," said Azlan. "You might have a concussion." Then, he pressed his hand to her forehead, his face full of concern. "And very likely a fever too."

Azlan dashed out of the room and reappeared with a bowl of what looked like a thin broth.

"Here."

Jay hesitated as she inspected the broth.

"Drink it," he ordered. "You'll feel better."

Jay obeyed and took a careful sip. But as soon as she swallowed the first few drops of the liquid, a flash of energy surged through her. She quickly guzzled down the drink, noticing that her pain was a distant memory.

"What is this?" Jay was genuinely surprised by the potency of the concoction.

"My mother used to cook this up for me when she worked in the labs up on the surface," said the man, dusting his hands as he settled back onto the chair. "Now, do you trust me enough to tell me what happened?"

Jay frowned. Could she trust this man? *Should* she trust this man? She had too many questions and not enough answers. All she wanted to do was to trust this man, but she knew she couldn't take any chances. It was her blind trust in everyone that got her in this mess in the first place.

"Okay, here's what," Azlan said. "You rest up and when you're ready to talk, we'll talk." Then, he left the room momentarily and returned with a glass of water. Jay watched him place it next to the lamp. Then, he looked at her sympathetically, smiled and left the room, leaving her alone with ample time to escape.

※ ※ ※

Jay was rummaging through the wires in Boro's back. The bot had been completely shut off. She needed him online fast. Frantically, the girl meddled with the wires, her eyes darting from the door and then back to the wires.

"Come on Boro, get up," she muttered as she nervously fidgeted around with the wires and finally kicked the bot. It worked.

"Jay?" Boro sounded unusually disoriented for a bot.

"Boro!" Jay put her hand on her mouth. She looked at the door. There was no sign of Azlan. She sighed with relief.

"Look, we need to hurry before Azlan comes."

"Who?" Boro scratched his metal head.

"Never mind! The *man*! You were right all along, Boro. This place is odd – the bots, the sky, even the humans. This is not the Gedrosia we were looking for. It's some freak facility." Jay was shaking as she said this. She rubbed her arms to make the goosebumps go away and stared at Boro with hooded, frightened eyes. "We need to get out of here now!"

"Jay, I hear you, but listen to me," Boro leaned forward. "We don't know our way out and we might get seen by those Jotuns again. They are after us and they won't hesitate to attack. Don't you understand?"

"We'll figure it out, but let's go before that man comes back," Jay was now tugging at the bot's arm while trying to keep her voice low. Then, she peeped outside the doorway to see if there was anyone there. With the coast clear, she tugged at Boro. "Come, get up and let's try to find our way out of here. He won't notice if we sneak out..."

"Jay, hold on. That man saved us! You might not remember, but he fought off the bots and then brought us here to safety," Boro paused. "Once you told him your name, he said he knew you."

"What are you talking about?" Jay frowned. She had no recollection of the conversation she had had with Azlan.

"Boro, let's discuss this after we get out of..." Before Jay could finish, Azlan appeared at the doorway with a tray of snacks and tea. "Thought you might be hungry Jay."

"Oh," Jay jerked around, scared and guilty at the same time. Azlan looked at her, confused at first, but quickly realized what her plan was.

"Look, you aren't a prisoner here." Azlan turned to Jay. "You're welcome to leave whenever you want, but you both are in deep trouble and this is the only place where you might be safe."

"No, its..." Her voice came out meek, more out of shame than fear. "I don't know what is going on here and who to trust."

Suddenly, it was hitting her all at once, the shock and loneliness of the last few days dawning on her, like small waves forming a tsunami. She began sobbing quietly, reflecting on all that had elapsed since she arrived in this place: the unusual bots, their quiet escape from the Compound, the uneasy couple that disappeared leaving them all alone, the abandoned site, and the rogue bots that attacked her. *Nothing was right; everything was wrong!*

"Do you want to tell me how you got here?" Azlan said softly.

"It's just… stupid. We came from Kolachi, followed some directions to this place expecting it to be some archaeological ruin. A few seconds later, we are being attacked by bots. Now, you come along," Jay looked up at him, "I have no idea who you are."

Azlan smiled at her sympathetically. "Listen, why don't you come outside to the pantry area. It's a bit airier than this room and we can all have something to eat. Perhaps, we can talk a bit. Deal?"

"Deal." And this time Jahan Jumander meant it.

***

"So, how'd you get here?" Azlan asked as he stood over the kitchen counter, preparing some tea.

Jay quickly realized they were in some kind of underground chamber with no skylight. The pantry and the living area was in a large dark cavern, lit up by pebble-shaped stones giving off light, bathing the cave in a purple glow. The room she had come out of was a small alcove of the cavern.

"Where are we and what are these?" Jay asked, as she touched the luminous walls.

Azlan grinned at the girl. "Naturally luminescent rocks within the Makran tunnels. I've used them to illuminate the home. Don't need no power. Plus, the gypsum that coats the cave walls reflects the light. Here, you take out a headlamp, an' this tunnel will fill up with bright light."

Azlan brought out a battery lamp and handed it over to Jay. She turned it on, and the entire place shimmered.

"Wow! So this is where you live?" she asked.

"Yes." Azlan answered nonchalantly. "Now, back to my question. How did you two get here? In fact, how'd you even know about Gedrosia?" Azlan sat down next to her on the table with mugs of tea.

Jay took one mug and raised it to thank him. Then she took a sip of the piping hot tea. "It all began in Kolachi..." she paused as opened up her backpack and took out her leatherbound journal, "This journal belongs to my father. He and my mother were well known archaeologists who disappeared in the Makran desert, looking for Gedrosia. I thought if I could trace their route, I'd find out what happened to them and where they disappeared. Maybe, get some closure," Jay pursed her lip, "but instead, I stumbled here."

"Stumbled here?" Azlan sounded bemused.

"Kind of, yes." Jay looked at Boro, then went on to explain everything that had happened in the last week: how she, Erol and Boro left Kolachi following the coordinates, how they were chased in the desert by some men in a black vehicle; how they had gotten separated; how she and Boro fell through the *dambani kaur*; how they met Oran and Mazu; how Mazu snuck them out of the Compound and took them to Raul and Delara; and how Raul and Delara disappeared unusually the following morning.

After everything, Azlan quietly stared at her as he rubbed his chin. "I see now."

Meanwhile, Boro interrupted his thinking. "Sir, if you don't mind my asking, why don't you live somewhere where there is skylight?" Boro asked.

Azlan rolled his eyes. "Of all the things to ask, this is what concerns you?"

"He has a point." Jay muttered. This place is kind of dingey. Why aren't you living with the other humans in the Res Complex?"

"Everything under the skylight is under surveillance. And I didn't like to be under surveillance."

"What's wrong with being under surveillance?" Jay asked.

"What's wrong?! You know what! Why don't you both let me ask you the questions. What did Oran and Mazu tell you about this place?"

"Hmm. Not much to be honest." Jay tried to recall everything Oran had told them. "We were told that this place was a research facility of some sort, to preserve living things?"

Azlan sighed. "Do you know about the HumanX Project?"

Jay hesitated. She had indeed heard about the project somewhere, but her memory was a bit fuzzy about what the project was actually about. She vaguely recalled learning something in her history class about a Volgan AI named ENO2 who had predicted human extinction following the loss of animal and plant biodiversity. It was after this that the Conservation Laws were enacted. The Laws prescribed an entirely austere form of living and as one can imagine, they were extremely controversial. Some even say the Bot Wars were a direct result of them.

"Wasn't the HumanX Project something that led to the Conservation Laws?" Jay said. "They were some kind of laws to protect our environment?"

"Well... sure," Azlan said though it was obvious he was displeased by the answer.

"The HumanX Project was an effort by many Units of the world to preserve biological diversity. This was so that we could drastically lower the probability of extinction of human beings, which was predicted to be 99% in five centuries."

"What?" Jay sounded surprised.

"He is saying that humans are predicted to go extinct in another 500 years." Boro repeated calmly.

"Well, it's now 450 years. And yes." Azlan said.

Jay tried to take deep breaths. "What about the Conservation Laws? They were going to remedy this right?"

Azlan laughed. "Those Laws were never supposed to work—they're just a coverup for the Sanctuaries."

Jay's mouth hung open as she rose from the table, dread filling up inside her like a helium balloon.

"Calm down, kid. I can't tell you anything if you start panicking." Azlan said calmly. "And it's all a scientific prediction with limitations. In any case, that's why the Interregional Union for Conservation of Humans and Bots, better known by its initials, the C.H.B. had been set up."

"CHB?" Jay asked, her forehead creasing. The acronyms sounded familiar, and then she remembered that she had heard them in relation to some peacekeeping effort in military-occupied Indus Unit during the Bot Wars. "Aren't they a peace-keeping body?"

"The CHB is a part of the United Regions if my processor serves me right." Boro answered before Azlan could.

"Yeah, it is, or rather it was. Now it is a Syndicate. Now, let me finish." Azlan gestured them both to be quiet. "So, in 2355, the CHB set up Gedrosia, a Sanctuary, to conserve biodiversity and conduct research to ensure that human beings do not in fact go extinct."

Jay hesitated before she spoke. "How come no one knows about the Sanctuaries and the CHB? And why is this place such a secret?"

Boro added in. "And how is it that there is no trace of Gedrosia in any computer database?"

Azlan turned to Boro. "Cause the CHB, it turns out, is shady. I mean they like to say that secrecy is important for their work, but it's all a ruse for their shady stuff."

"What shady stuff are you talking about?" Jay looked at him sceptically.

Azlan shook his head and waved his hand. "Look, I've already said too much. This place is complicated. There're secrets. Far too many to count."

Jay leaned forward. "That's what Raul told me too. What do you mean by secrets? What secrets are you guys talking about?"

"Secrets that don't concern you! You're already in a lot of trouble."

"Urgghh" Jay stomped her feet. "Why won't anyone tell me what's going on and why we're in trouble in the first place?"

Boro added. "Jay's right. We deserve answers."

Azlan paused considering something. "There's no going back, orite?"

"Yes, we know," Jay said. "Begin from the start. Like I did."

Azlan stood up and began to pace back and forth. "Listen very carefully then, Jay and Boro. Sanctuaries like Gedrosia started off with the *right* motives – to preserve plants and animals yada yada. Then, the CHB became a Syndicate some years back to be able to benefit from more funding. Years passed and the Syndicate grew to become a secretive and greedy organization, unchecked by the UR," Azlan paused, then returned to his seat. "We don't know what triggered this change, who's responsible, and when it all began – but we do know that since then, the CHB Syndicate has started to finance a great deal of illegal, heck unethical research in its sanctuaries."

Jay laughed but Azlan kept a serious expression.

"What kind of research are you talking about?" Boro asked.

"Well, to begin with, it is quite obvious that they're enhancing bot lines, even though that has been outlawed."

"We could tell that from a mile away." Boro stated in a self-congratulatory tone.

Jay added. "But that's not so bad, is it?"

"Yeah, enhancements aren't the issue, Jay. There's something more..." Azlan paused trying to thing of the right word, "*sinister* going on here."

"Sinister? What do you mean?" Jay asked.

Azlan took out a cigarette. "Do you mind?"

Jay nodded. "Sure, go ahead."

Azlan took a whiff. "We think that the bots have been Transformed through introduction of organic matter from animals, which mind you, is unethical. We also suspect experimentation on humans without their consent." He took another whiff and calmly stared at them both. "This puts into question the entire nature and ethics of their research not to mention accountability and transparency."

Jay had never heard of Transformations of bots - the merging of bot and organic matter.

"Transformations are highly illegal," Boro remarked. "How could the CHB get away with something like this without the world knowing?"

Azlan made an I-don't-know gesture. "I wish I could tell you. Lots of people asked the same question, and now they're all missing."

Jay gulped. "What are you trying to say?"

Azlan sighed. "Kid, my advice is not to ask any questions or else you'll get yourself killed."

"Killed? "Jay let out a panicked reply. "Can't we just have a normal conversation please? No one has to get killed."

"Look, it's late. Definitely past your bedtime," Azlan looked at his watch, "We'll talk more about this in the morning."

"No, but we need to-"

"Missy, you need to sleep! Now come! You can take the bedroom in the den, and I'll sleep here in the cavern." He prodded

125

her back into the bedroom that she was in before. Boro followed her.

"Next time, don't take on a fight unless you think you can win," Azlan said as he yawned "cuz you don' understand what's really going on."

Jay looked back at Azlan, her eyes frowning, and hands on her waist. "Why are you still holding back on the truth?"

"Tomorrow, I'll tell you more, little one," Azlan said, half-amused by Jay's feisty nature. "For now, get rest."

Without letting her talk any further, Azlan closed the door behind leaving Jay and Boro alone in the bedroom.

"Oh Boro! All of this is a little too crazy, even for me." Jay said, as she jumped into the bed.

"I agree with you, and I am afraid that it might only get crazier," Boro sat beside her and put his arm around her shoulder.

Jay turned to him. "Why do you think so? Why is it going to get crazier?"

"Oh, just intuition," Boro said.

"Bots have intuition?" Jay asked.

Boro didn't answer but had an impish grin across his metal face. Jay looked at him in confusion, then rested her head on his shoulder.

"What does your intuition say about Erol? Do you think he is okay?" she asked, as she stared out the window at the alien planet she was on, wondering how long she had been her. Two days now, but it felt like a lifetime. She missed her bed in the hostel, but she missed Erol most of all.

Boro smiled at her. "My dear, I really hope so."

CHAPTER 15

Journey into Gedrosia

The school cafeteria had just served high-tea at the University of Panjgur: a meal of fried onions, potatoes and banana tots. A very hungry professor and a street kid from Kolachi made their way to the cafeteria to satiate their tummies. After fuelling themselves with sufficient caffeine, they proceeded to the Archaeology Lab to gather some gadgets for their imminent journey.

At 4:00 pm in the afternoon of a sunny July day, the only sad soul working in the lab, glued to his computer was Faruk, a diligent PhD. student studying ancient Balochi scripts and developing a program to parse the scripts.

"Faruk, what are you still doing here?" Salim asked, somewhat annoyed to see someone in his lab.

"Sir, I was fixing some bugs in the code –"

Salim glared at him. "I know *that*. I mean, what are you doing in the lab, this time of the day!? Why haven't you gone home yet?" The professor wiped his forehead with a napkin and tried to maintain his cool, a skill that had taken him a few years of teaching to master.

By now, the student was shaking and Erol felt a bit sorry for him. He was probably a few years older than him and yet, looked as frightened as his five-year-old nephew when he was caught committing some mischievous act.

"Uh... sir... no one is around in the dorms, and I gathered I could work a bit extra this summer." There was a pause and then a sigh. "I mean I really cannot afford to go back to Laroe this year."

The professor wasn't nearly as touched as Erol was. Perhaps, he had seen too many sad souls in his life as a professor. Perhaps, he was used to hearing the sob stories of the numerous orphans or troubled kids roaming around on campus.

"Never mind Faruk. I have an important mission coming up and I think I can use an extra hand. Are you interested in field trips?"

Faruk looked at the professor, hesitating to answer, "Uh sir, not really. I like to code..."

"Continue coding on the hack software you were developing. I think it might come in handy on our field trip?"

"The hack software?" Erol was confused by the exchange.

The professor glanced at him. "The hack software is designed to breach security and access databases."

"But you're an archaeologist," Erol scratched his head. "I thought you were doing research on ancient scripts."

"Erol, my boy. These days, all the knowledge of the past including ancient scripts is kept safely hidden from the public in restricted encrypted databases. As researchers, we often need to get to the truth which at times requires going through some illegal channels."

Erol rubbed his neck again. "If you say so. I mean I don't mind hacking and breaking the law, but you're a professor."

"Oh, it's harmless. We've used it only a few times to access restricted information from the Ministry of Ancient Artifacts. Now, where were we? Yes, Faruk, are you ready?"

"But sir...."

"You will get ten extra points on your final grade."

128

Faruk's eyes lit up. "Sure, Dr. Salim. Where are we going, Sir?"

"The Makran," Salim replied, as a smile spread across his face, "You're interested, right?"

"Yes, certainly!" Faruk exclaimed while mumbling under his breath, "Grades, yes..."

The conversation ended briskly as the professor brushed past the boy and ran to the desks, scanning through the cabinets and drawers and hoarded some strange-looking devices and tablets. His eyes were shining brilliant, clearly suggestive of his excitement over the impending journey. He looked at Erol, "You have a vehicle?"

Erol nodded. "Jay's Tezla jeep. It's parked out front."

"Hmm, too big. We will take my vehicle." The professor then turned to Faruk. "Boy, you have no qualms about tight spaces, do you?"

Faruk shook his head. "No sir."

"Then we are ready! Faruk, go grab the hackpad, GeoNav, extra power and maybe even the plasma rifle from my office."

Faruk scratched his head. "The plasma rifle..."

"Just the long pole-looking device near my desk."

Faruk nodded and quickly disappeared.

Erol rubbed the back of his neck, a little confused by the exchange that had taken place, as well as Salim's plans.

"Dr. Salim, why are we taking all this stuff and what was all that about tight spaces?"

"Son, so many questions! We'll be taking my Compactor so we can get further in to Gedrosia. And it can be a bit cramped. I don't want any of you to be puking in it!"

"The Compact-what?" Erol asked. "Why would we puke? And you didn't answer my other questions."

But the professor was busy in other thoughts. He was scavenging through his drawers, and when he finally emerged successful—holding out some papers– he was on his way out the back door of the lab room. For a moment, Erol and Faruk just stood there, frozen as they watched the excited professor leave.

But the professor's bald head emerged from the door. "Well, what're you both waiting for? Come on! Follow me."

The two shook their heads and quickly followed the professor outside. They continued down the sidewalk in the back, where the professor revealed his vehicle. It was an extremely compact, human-sized pod.

"A pod?" Erol was surprised to see a pod that small.

"Not a pod," Salim replied, dryly. "This is a Compacter. These beauties are designed to go into places that most vehicles can't go.

"Where *are* we going?" asked Erol and Faruk, almost in unison, as they both exchanged confused looks.

"Down under, boys!"

✳ ✳ ✳

A curious looking pod appeared on the Panjgur highway, causing a stir in the road traffic. Vehicles were slowing down, the eyes of the passengers veering in the direction of the Compactor— instead of on the road. Even the mecha road police seemed confused, their metal eyes flickering at the sight of the unusually small vehicle. After all, there were no protocols on how to manage such a pod on regular traffic. Inside, one could see three people crushed into the tiny pod, a balding professor, a young and excited teenager, and another excited young person, except in the case of the latter, it was the kind of excitement that one calls 'very nervous.'

The Compactor took an hour to get out of the city, battling its way through the cramped roads and competing with all kinds of traffic to funnel out of the town. As the trio drove through the city, Erol was able to squeeze his head to one corner to catch a good look at the city of Panjgur in its full glory. The sun had begun its descent and one by one, the solar road lights turned on, illuminating the highway. Signs of progress and development were evident everywhere as they drove under a web of overpasses. Construction was going on at all levels, and a large holosign floated above the city announcing the 'New Bullet Train to Gandhara.' Unlike Turbat and Gwadar, Panjgur had bounced back quickly from the Bot Wars.

After funnelling out of the main Panjgur highway, the rest of the journey remained traffic-free and uneventful. The only excitement the trio encountered was construction work on the road that required a detour. Thus, instead of the main highway that Erol had taken, the trio went further inland going in through unpaved, mud roads and passing by several fascinating towns, or rather their remnants.

By evening, they were traveling through the sandy wastelands of Makran, the stark lifelessness of the desert leaving even the sparkly-eyed professor somewhat gloomy. And with night fast approaching and the horizon already red with dusk, the trio decided it was time to stop and camp, resting through the night.

The next morning, as early as the first sign of light, the party arose and pushed on. A night's rest had done them good and they were in a more talkative and festive mood. Salim discoursed on the need for reviving archaeology in the Indus Unit while Faruk surprisingly argued for more field trips for students.

By afternoon, they had made it through the central Makran, the temperatures soaring into the high nineties. Despite this, the pod, with its thin glass cover, was comfortable, insulated from outside temperatures.

"Dr. Salim?" Erol asked, his nose pressed against the glass of the pod and not out of choice

"Yes, Erol."

"How is the Compactor able to stay so cool? Even with all of us stuffed in it."

"Well... it's uniquely designed for underground terrains."

Erol turned and gave the professor a funny look. "Are you really serious about underground terrains?"

"I am always serious. When have I joked around with you kids?"

Erol raised his brows as the professor settled back in his seat, watching the hot heavy air run over the window while managing to stay cool.

As the journey progressed, the landscape made its shift from sandy dunes to arid flatland by mesas. From their navigation screen on the Compactor, it was evident that they were very close to their final destination.

In a matter of hours, the trio was at the base of the plateau that bore the numerous mud mounds. Salim flicked some controls on the Compactor and then manoeuvred the pod as it made its steep and slow ascent. At the top, they could view the myriad of little mounds, no more than one or two feet high, dotting the plateau. There was no vegetation, simply an empty expanse of foreign formations.

"This is incredible!" Faruk stared at the mounds starry-eyed.

"These are mud volcanoes," the professor said while surveying the area from his pod. "They're known as the *dambani kaur*." As he scanned the area, his eye finally rested on the largest of the mounds. "And that is the largest one!"

"That also looks like the one that Jay and Boro were inspecting." Erol rubbed his head. "How did you know?"

But the professor ignored his question and was already working his way around the area.

"Where are you going, Dr.?" Erol asked, watching the professor stand at the edge of the mound, digging away with his hands. Finally, he looked back at Erol and Faruk smiling at them all, "Hey guys, give me a hand and bring the pod, will you? We gotta go."

"Go where?"

"Underground. Both of you, in the Compactor. Now!"

Erol and Faruk looked confused, as they sat snug in the Compactor. The professor joined them. "Any time now."

"What are we waiting for, Dr. Salim?" Erol began to wonder whether the professor had perhaps gone mad.

"We are going down, my dear boy."

"Down? What are you even saying Sir?" Faruk exchanged a quick glance with Erol, who was beginning to really think the professor was mad.

"Have you ever been in quicksand, Erol?"

"I haven't and I wouldn't ever want to –"

Before Erol could complete his sentence, a strong wind surrounded the Compactor and the ground beneath them sank as if it never existed.

Everything around them went dark and for a moment, all of them, along with the Compactor, were falling into a wide sandy tunnel, the walls graphite in appearance. When they slowed down, an incline became visible.

A loud thud, then a bump. They were in a dark cave.

They were in Gedrosia.

***

In the gathering twilight of dusk, Salim entered the familiar underground city of Gedrosia with his group of younglings. Slowly, he got out of the Compactor and inspected how the place had changed. A simulated sky had replaced the dark rock ceiling, the boundary rocks were now gentle hills fading into the sky and the Ghaba was alive with sounds of scurrying animals and chirping birds. The rumours were true then – the underground cavernous sanctuary had transformed into a virtual Elysium. The original Gedrosia, the grand sanctuary, grandest of the Syndicate, was lost in the simulated facades and holographic overlays.

Salim turned to his young companions and knew he had to make sure they stayed well out of sight. After all, he'd been timely informed by Mazu of the risks of coming to Gedrosia and the orders to stay out of the Syndicate's eyes. Fortunately, he knew his way around, and he remembered the forest and the path leading to the Dark Ghaba and to the secret shack. Getting there would be easy enough especially with the Compacter, which had made it through the portal as designed.

Without much further ado, Salim drove the Compacter with its tightly packed passengers around the forest's edge. They made their way through Pine Grove and the Ghaba until the thicket of trees surrounded them like a dense blanket of darkness. And the sky above them grew dark, so dark that it was like night.

After they'd covered some distance, Salim parked the Compacter behind a bushel. Without so much as a murmur, he took out his orblight and along with Erol and Faruk quietly got off and travelled through the Dark Ghaba. And it was dark because unlike the rest of Gedrosia, this part of the Ghaba had no virtual sky. Up above was a ceiling of pure rock. But no questions were to be asked until they were out of sight – that was the agreement. Until then, Erol and Faruk remained silent, following the professor as quietly as they could.

With Salim in the lead, they went deeper and deeper until the forest swallowed them whole. Their only source of light was the orb that allowed them to see a small perimeter. But as they continued in further, the forest thinned out. As they broke through a less dense part of the forest, a small dirt track became visible.

Down the track they went, finally arriving at a small wooden shack lit up by luminescent rock. The shack was camouflaged by ferns and moss. It was run-down, with a creaky door for an entrance.

All three of them entered the shack. It was dingy and windowless, lit by a single plasma flame dangling from the low ceiling. A faint smell of rotten leaves lingered about the place. Wooden filing cabinets stood around the walls; from their labels, it looked like they contained details of some experiments and observations of the forest. Faruk grabbed one of the files from the cabinet and began shuffling through the pages.

"Wow," he muttered, "ancient relics . . . species preservations . . ." he turned to the professor. "Perhaps I can get access to some more scripts. This will be so great for my research!" Without any hint of restraint, he retrieved a large roll of parchment from one of the drawers and stretched it out in front of him.

"Don't touch it!" scolded the professor, as he grabbed the parchment from Faruk. "We're not here to mess around with the place. We came here on a mission, and we leave as quickly and quietly as possible." But even as the command rang out, Faruk continued scanning the shack, his eyes sparkling with curiosity.

"What's the plan from here?" Erol asked.

"My boy, the plan is for you to rest while Faruk and I finish off on his hack software so that we can find Jay and leave undetected."

"So when do we start searching for Jay?" Erol asked, eyes full of genuine concern, "Any time we waste is time that Jay remains in peril!"

"It's too dark to look for her right now. In the morning, I have to meet with some people to get briefed and once I'm back, we will look for her."

Erol rubbed his neck. "But are you at least going to tell us about this place?"

The professor, seeing the boy's growing frustration decided to say the obvious.

"Like I told you before, this place is called Gedrosia, where Jay's parents and I used to work. It was originally designed to be a sanctuary to preserve living creatures. Now however…"

"Yes?"

"Now, this place is dangerous. Very dangerous. So the fewer questions you ask, the better it is for you."

The professor's statement left a foreboding feeling among the two boys, who remained silent, following along with orders and proceeding to prepare for the night, full of uncertainty.

CHAPTER 16

Revelations

In all his fifty years, it had never occurred to Azlan to give some thought as to how he ended up in his hermitage in Gedrosia. He remembered it as a succession of events from the death of his mother to a scholarship to study geological engineering. As soon as he graduated, he remembered being whisked away by some fancy-clad people who recruited him to work on the 'most important mission of the next millennium'. Yes, that is how he came to be in Gedrosia. Little did he know then that there would be no turning back.

Today, though, he took some time to look back on his life and question every decision he had made, particularly his most recent blunder: bringing home the teenage daughter of his long-missing friend and her bot, especially when both had targets on their head.

Azlan sighed. How was he supposed to remain a hermit when the most wanted people in Gedrosia were occupants of his home? But Azlan's moment of contemplation was short-lived. He turned around when he heard the knock on the door. It was Jay. She peeped in through the half-open door. "Can I come in?"

Azlan nodded as Jay tiptoed inside the room. She examined the room, a cliché reflection of a bachelor's abode: Dust everywhere, tapestries rotting on the walls, books scattered on the sofa. It was worse than Erol's dorm room.

"Bots don't offer cleanin' services here," Azlan grinned at her. "What are you doing up so early?"

"Couldn't sleep any more than I did," she said. She frowned, moving closer. "You look a little pensive today. Is everything okay?"

Azlan pursed his lips, then nodded. "Yeah, everythin's fine. Don't worry about me." He smiled and got up from his chair, "Come outside and eat some breakfast."

Jay followed Azlan outside into the lounge chamber where Boro was already awaiting them, alert. Azlan flicked his eyebrows at him, then made his way towards the kitchen counter.

"Did you sleep well though?" he asked Jay, as he poured some water into a rusty kettle and placed it on the stove.

"I did. No scary dreams at least," Jay replied cheerfully, as she took a seat on the kitchen table beside Boro. "What about you?"

"Eh. I don't dream for some reason."

Azlan preoccupied himself in the kitchen as he rummaged through his cupboards trying to look for ingredients he hadn't used in a while. Jay looked at him and wondered if they were his only visitors in a while. Heck, looking at the state of his home, they were probably the only visitors *ever*.

As soon as the kettle began to whistle, Azlan poured a pink-coloured tea into giant cups and brought those over to Jay. He took a seat beside her and remained contemplative. When sufficient time had elapsed, he took a deep breath.

"Look kid. You asked me a lot of questions yesterday – and you know what, it's quite refreshing. Truth is, we all don't know what's going on with the Syndicate, and we don't have a clue how to expose them." A pause. "And the thing is, even if there's evidence to expose the Syndicate, many of us don't think it's worth it. To go against them."

Boro folded his arms. "How don't you know anything about the organization you work for, the organization you've sworn an oath of secrecy to?"

Jay shook her head. "Boro's right. You must know something about the Syndicate and what's it doing? And if you don't, why aren't you all asking questions?"

Azlan frowned. "Because asking questions has gotten folks in trouble. And also, even with all its problems, the Syndicate is the best chance we have to ensure mankind's survival. If it gets shut down, then that's the end. For everyone. Those Overground governments are ignoring the certainty of the ENO2 predictions, not to mention preventing the enhancement of bots. Without the help of bots and advanced AI, we're doomed, truly. Scientists here are trying to worry about long term human preservation, rather than tryin' to fight a structure that is committing some... petty crimes."

"Petty crimes?" Jay paused. "If that's all there is to it, why are you telling me this and getting worked up?" Jay asked.

Azlan was sweating. His breath was coming in deep. He took a long deep breath. "You know what? I don't know, kid. I don't know." For a moment, all of them were quiet.

Jay finally piped up. "Look, I'm sorry for all the questions. I'm still trying to understand all this. But maybe I don't need to. I'm an outsider, and hopefully, I can get out of here soon enough. That's all I want - to be back home with my friends and what remains of my family."

"Yeah, about that." Azlan grumbled under his breath. "I have to figure out something, because it won't be easy to get you out of here."

"But Mazu is already figuring that out?" Jay said.

"But you both are right now under my care. I will speak to Mazu to see what is being done about getting you both back home."

"We can help you figure it out." Jay blurted.

"Shush, you'll only get us in more trouble. Just no more questions, otherwise you'll end up like Urmir -" Azlan suddenly stopped himself, slapping his mouth shut.

"Urmir?" Jay had stiffened at the mention of the name. She wondered if this was the same person she'd thought of. She tried to keep her voice calm. "Urmir who?"

Azlan looked her in the eye, then exhaled. "Urmir Jumander."

The words from his mouth were stone cold arrows piercing deep into Jay, and for a second, the girl had to remind herself to breathe.

"Urmir Jumander," Jay's voice came out meek and trembling, "That's my father's name!"

✸✸✸

For a second, everything remained still, as if time itself was on pause. Jay could hear her ears ringing. When the ringing finally stopped, she turned to Azlan, her voice trembling. "How do you know my father, Azlan?"

Azlan shifted his eyes around and could see the frustration in Jay's face. He sighed. "I owe you an explanation, Jay. Your father, he was no ordinary archaeologist." Another deep sigh. "He was one of the founding members of Gedrosia"

Jay let out a frightened laugh. "What are you talking about? Is this some kind of joke?" Even as she said this, she had her hand on her chest and could hear her heart was beating so loud she thought she was going to have a heart attack. "He was just an archaeologist..."

"Look, kid. It seems like they never told you anything." Azlan grumbled something under his breath, then turned to Jay. "Your parents, they were famous. We all knew 'em." Azlan sighed deeply.

"Your father and mother were recruited to set up Gedrosia thirty years ago."

Jay couldn't believe what she was hearing. Her mind was in a fog of confusion. Soon enough, tears had formed in her eyes. "What are you saying?"

Boro stood beside her, patting her shoulder as the girl sobbed. "Azlan, can you please tell explain how Jay's parents could have been involved in Gedrosia when they were actually archaeologists."

Azlan turned to the bot. "That's precisely why they were recruited for the mission, Boro. Jay's parents were the best archaeologists in the Unit. They knew these wastelands so well."

Jay was trying to hold back the stream of tears now flowing down her cheeks. "If that's true, I would know. They left a journal for me, and they said they worked on excavations. They wouldn't have kept this a secret from me. They just *couldn't* have."

"Oh, but they did, Jay!" Azlan paused and leaned closer to her. "And they had to keep this a secret from you I suspect, for your own safety."

"My safety? Why?"

"Your parents were the ones leading this mission, but at some point, your father wanted to leave this place. That is when the trouble started."

"What trouble? What happened to my parents?"

Azlan looked at her for a while, then gulped. "I am not sure. We all know that your parents had a disagreement with the higher-ups. Then, they disappeared. They went missing some eleven years ago, never to be seen again in Gedrosia or the Overground. Don't ask because no one knows what happened to them."

"So, is there a chance that they are alive then?" Jay asked although instantly regretted asking the question.

Azlan's face dropped. "I can't be certain, but I don't think they are alive. Most people believe that the Syndicate did something to them."

The answer left her frozen. Jay tried to process the deep sinking feeling inside of her. She was angry, lost and grief-stricken, all at once.

"Why didn't I ever know?"

Azlan, expecting tears to follow, leaned closer and took her in his embrace. "Probably because your parents wanted to keep you safe and away from this place. They would *rather* see you alive than never see you at all. The only reason you are alive at this very moment is because your parents had to pay a very heavy price, a dear sacrifice."

Jay sniffed and wiped her years. Instantly, she knew what she had to do. She had to find a way to expose the Syndicate and their crimes. If they were the reason for her parents' death, she would have her revenge. Whatever the stakes.

Jay got up, her hands rolled up in a fist, resolution dawning in her eyes. "Azlan, I will need your help."

"With what?"

"Help me defeat the Syndicate."

Azlan chuckled. "Get in line. So many of us do."

"Yeah, but all we need to do is gather some evidence to expose them."

"So, you want to make the same mistake as your parents? They wanted to expose the Syndicate and look what happened there,"

Jay's eyes welled up again. He was right. What was she thinking? "Then, what do I do? I am already in danger here, and I might just be stuck forever. At least I should complete what my parents couldn't." Jay burst out in tears as she considered her situation.

142

Azlan grabbed hold off her shoulders. "Look kid. You only have one option, and that is to focus on getting out. If what you've told me is true, Mazu is probably working his magic to get you out of here. I'll try to meet with him, and we will figure out a way to get you home. In the meanwhile, you stay out of trouble and stop asking nosy questions that will get you in more trouble."

Boro stepped forward. "Even if you manage to get us out, what is the chance that we will be safe? The CHB may continue to pursue us."

"Because you have no role to play in Gedrosia." Azlan calmly said. "And a lot has changed since then. The CHB would not be interested in pursuing you. In any case, right now, you need to leave this situation to the adults."

Azlan disappeared into the bedroom and returned having donned a long brown cloak.

"Are we going somewhere?" Jay asked.

"Not we. Me. You both stay here. I'm going to try to meet with Mazu and figure out a way to get you both back home safely." Azlan smiled as he made his way through a large iron door at the end of the cavern.

"I'll be back soon."

With that, he left the Jay and Boro in his cavern, a loud clang resounding behind him.

***

As soon as Azlan was out of his chambers, he scurried through the low tunnels to arrive at an open cavern. Without much time wasted, he looked around to make sure of complete privacy, and then took out a comms device, tapping the **SECRET** label on his contact list. He heard the ring go by three times unanswered. Then someone answered.

"Mazu? It's Azlan." Azlan spoke without waiting for the other person to answer.

On the other end was a slight groan. "You should have been more careful."

It was Mazu. "Should have waited for me to answer."

"Don't have time." Azlan whispered.

"The hermit doesn't have time?" Mazu almost chuckled. "This must be important. What is it about, Azlan?"

"It's about the girl. She's with me." Azlan replied. "You know. Jumander's daughter."

Mazu exhaled, what was quite noticeably a sound of relief. "Thank goodness! Raul and Delara had to go somewhere…" A slight pause. "Are they safe?"

"They are. Where did Raul and Delara go?"

Another pause. "Never mind that. They're on an important mission and need to lay low for a while. The girl, Jahan Jumander, however, is not safe here anymore." We must get her out of here. And it's finally time to execute out plan…" Mazu's voice trailed off in rambling words that were inaudible.

"Wait a minute, you're cutting out." Azlan said. "What plan are you talking about? *The* plan? We aren't ready."

"Well, yes. Perhaps, but opportunity has presented itself." A slight hesitation followed. "Listen, perhaps it's best I discuss this in person with you. Can you meet me at Mariner's Edge?"

There was a pause. Azlan didn't want to be away from home too long. He turned around to see the tunnels leading to his home. They were quiet. Jay and Boro should be okay there. He turned to the phone.

"Are you still there, Azlan?" Mazu asked.

"I'm on my way."

CHAPTER 17

Oran / Aklan

Oran examined the stranger's face. His red eyes glittered behind transparent seals of biological membranes. Suture lines traversed the skull, concealed by strong, but malleable metal plates which could easily take the shape of any expression. Holes were puckered for the ears and nostrils. Dark thoughts floated in his mind, as Oran assessed the stranger. He had been observing him regularly, noticing each detail of this evolving visage. The metamorphosis was complete now—more than complete, in fact. The stranger was fully formed—with only a thin layer of reflective surface separating Oran from his own former self.

The cyborg blinked, as the film cleared from his eyes. He had to remind himself that the image he was seeing now was his own image, a reflection of his hybridization. But still, he wondered if his loyalties were with bots, or with humans?

Or neither. Oran grinned widely. His plan was working perfectly. He was unrecognizable, his past sins erased and he could start from a blank slate. His previous face and body would exist only as a memory and that too, will soon be erased, forgotten over time. The memory which had tormented him for long days and longer nights could now be purged from his thoughts.

And he was glad he agreed to the Syndicate's deal. Of course, he suffered some inconvenience along the way but he was always willing to take a gamble. Besides, he had always hedged his bets—covered them both ways. If he had chosen to remain as Idris, his former human self, death would be a certainty. And with the option to give up his body for experimentation, he had managed to evade death altogether. In fact, his past sins would have led him to die a painful death, either in prison or in the real world. But he was smart. His plan had an elegant complexity beneath its apparent simplicity. Quite ingenious. All by volunteering himself to science.

Oran's real name was Idris Aklan. Idris had been a bot mechanic in Laroe. He was gifted in the mechanical sciences and discovered by a professor at the University of Indus Sciences, who trained him to become the most renowned scientist in the Silk Road Region, in fact, the world. Except the world couldn't take his success. They refused to acknowledge his work, deeming his methodological approaches as illegal, inhumane even. He was tried for murdering a human, although, in his eyes, he gave that human immortality. And finally, they called him an infidel trying to play God. That was the end of his research.

Back in Laroe, there were mobs that began to threaten his family. By then, he knew he knew he had to get out. And he had figured out the perfect escape: Gedrosia. But there were plans to be made yet.

Oran couldn't rid himself of the nagging guilt that he felt for making this gamble. He sold not just himself, but his entire family to the Syndicate, in exchange for protection. His wife and daughter, who refused to join them in Gedrosia were murdered by the mob. Idris had no one now, but his own army of bots. That's what the Syndicate thought would help humanity survive; to become one with the machines.

He still wanted revenge, but from whom, he wasn't sure. He wanted his memories to be wiped out, but how could he? Who would remember his family? He looked down, but the stranger told him to look up.

It was too late. He could not stop anything. He inspected the body, a strange body that stood before him: tall and metallic; hard and wiry. He touched his head. *Two Brains.* One human, one bot.

The stranger smiled as the red light gleamed from his eyes, darkening to purple. Oran shuddered thinking of what madness lay within this man, this cyborg.

The cyborg turned towards the door, then paused and thought of his flashing past life. Then, he felt Idris disappear from his life altogether.

CHAPTER 18

Sanctuary Alert

"Tomas, this doesn't look good."

Moira Harper, the UR Premier was seated on her desk, staring dolefully at the blue envelope in front of her. It was an anonymous message calling for an investigation into the CBH Syndicate. And the unique crescent-shaped emblem on the envelope suggested it was indeed from the Gedrosian sanctuary itself.

"We need to investigate this Tomas. This is a message from trusted members of the sanctuary."

Tomas Adim was now considerably past his middle age and on his way to retiring as the Indus Unit Envoy. But he had now been offered a new role as Moira Harper's advisor, given that she herself was raised in the Indus Unit. Adim cleared his throat as he stared at her with concern. "Moira, I would also take this very seriously. In fact, there have been other concerns about Gedrosia…."

Adim paused and turned to his subordinate, a much younger officer who went by the name of Klaus Kahn. Kahn was in training to become the next Envoy for the Indus Unit. Tomas gestured to the boy to speak, and Moira gave another nod.

"Ma'am, some prominent scientists in Gedrosia would like to have an acquaintance with you," said Kahn as he shuffled uncomfortably in the seat across from her. "Senior scientists in Gedrosia are voicing concerns…."

"What concerns are we talking about?" Moira folded her arms, her eyes set in a deep furrow as he leaned against the desk.

"Illegal enhancements"

"Ah." The reply was not one of surprise but of expectation. Rumours were going around that the Syndicate was betraying the sanctuary mission, and instead channelling its money into bot enhancements. All hope for humanity would be lost if steps were not taken to hold them accountable.

"What generations are we talking about?" Moira asked.

Kahn scratched his head. There was no simple way to break this to the Premier. He turned to the Envoy.

Adim cleared his throat again. "Moira, it's no longer in bot domain anymore. It's now cybor-" the Envoy bit his lip immediately as he saw the colour fade away from the Premier's face.

"Are you sure, Tomas? Transformations are strictly prohibited, and we have some fantastic people in Gedrosia who would *never* allow this to happen."

"You mean Salim?"

Moira blushed.

Adim crossed his arms. "He's no longer working at Gedrosia, Moira. He's a tenured professor at the University of Panjgur."

"What! He left?"

There was surprise, mixed with hurt. Moira took some time to recover from the initial shock of this information, and then turned to Adim trying not to display any emotions.

"Did you speak to the CHB about the members of the Syndicate that are allowing this to happen?"

"Well, no." Tomas Adim answered, then signalled Kahn to talk.

"Ma'am. The thing is, now, the CHB *is* the Syndicate – and all members are aware of the activities going on in the sanctuaries."

"Are you saying the entire CHB is complicit in this?"

"Perhaps, ma'am. I can't be sure, but I will be investigating further."

Moira Harper was now off her chair, pacing back and forth, hand on her forehead. Knowing that this could well become a full-blown panic attack if she didn't control it, she returned to her seat and took deep breaths until she had calmed down.

"Tomas, what are we going to do?"

"Well, I have already taken some measures to address this issue. I only brought this up to you now because I had to sift truth from rumours."

"I see," Moira was lost in her thoughts, "you have moles to find out if what this letter indicates is true."

The Envoy hinted a smile. "I do have a few moles."

"Alright. Make sure that this remains between us," she walked over to order some tea for herself. "I'll expect you to verify everything soon especially about the Syndicate. So much seems to be happening without my knowledge. Salim and I used to communicate rather freely about the Sanctuaries back in the days. That was before I took on such a public role...." Moira was lost in thought for a second and then resumed. "Anyways, I need to know everything before things take a turn for the worst."

Thomas Adam and Klaus Kahn gave her a nodding bow as they left the room.

PART III

The Conflict

CHAPTER 19

Salim's Reunion

At the earliest hints of dawn, Professor Salim Sarmo was awake, preparing to leave the shack. Quietly, he snuck out the door, leaving his Compactor behind, then travelled on foot along the outskirts of the Dark Ghaba, orblight in hand. He stared up at the trees, their ancient canopy tops reaching out to pierce the rock ceiling. What a marvel, he thought to himself. Then, he retraced the steps to the entrance of the Makran tunnels, the path still etched in his mind from eons ago.

So much of Gedrosia was indeed the same as how he last left it: the craggy hills that circled the forest and the karst terrain, the Dark Ghaba which had stood the test of time, the secret shack and the Makran tunnels still well-preserved and hidden from the Compound's sight. In all this time, after more than thirty years, Gedrosia and its facades appeared to be the same. He hoped that his friends were the same too.

After passing through an avenue of gravel paths, Salim came across a plain of empty bedded stone, which ended only where the hills began. At the fringes, some unusually large boulders lay scattered about in sporadic fashion. Salim walked towards them. Finally, he approached a large stone boulder standing more than eight feet tall, right next to the hill. It did not need moving. It was already out of place, and the discoloured stone wall behind it already had loose stones. It looked like someone had passed through the entrance recently. He pushed the stone until a holographic keypad appeared. It asked for a 4-digit passcode.

There was no way he would know this passcode. Salim thought for a minute. What could the four numbers be? Then, he took out his tablet and read the message he received from Mazu earlier. *"At the eastern edge of the forest, go straight ahead towards the lignite boulder. Push it aside. Enter and turn right. Wait at the alcove."*

There was no passcode. Salim cursed himself but before he knew it, a metal hand appeared on his shoulder, startling him. Salim jumped and turned around to see a large bot carrying a cardboard box.

"Mazu, it's you!"

"Indeed, it is!" Mazu took Salim in a warm embrace. "I am glad you got my message. Did you come alone?"

"No, I have two boys with me. They're safe, back at the shack."

"Two boys?" Mazu asked. "Not the smartest move, Salim. But I'm sure you covered your tracks when you came here."

"I did. And I'll be out of your hairs as soon as I get my goddaughter, Jahan."

"Well, you will be pleased to know she is safe. For now."

"Phew," Salim sighed with relief. This rescue mission might be smoother than he expected. They'd be home in no time. He pointed at the cave. "Well then, let's get this meeting over with?"

Mazu grinned at him and typed in some digits, which fortunately opened up the door. "Here we go."

The two of them entered the cave, turning right through the tunnels, until the walls grew obsidian, reminders of a bygone era. Finally, they arrived at a dark alcove.

"Where is he?" Mazu muttered to himself.

"Where's who?"

But Mazu was walking up ahead to the alcove, where the shadow of a tall figure lurked. Finally, the person stepped forward in the dusky light and revealed himself to be Azlan.

"What are you doing here Salim?" Azlan asked in disbelief.

"I...I...none of your business. What are *you* doing here?" Salim said awkwardly.

Mazu cleared his throat. "Both of you, stop. I wanted both of you to meet me."

"Why?" Azlan stepped forward. "What's going on?"

Salim also stepped forward in unison, his chest high.

"Friends, the time has come. We have to stop the Syndicate. I have been able to gather some initial proof that the Syndicate has refocused their funding on enhancements and Transformations. And I have drafted communication for the UR, that we need someone else to lead the sanctuaries now."

"Transformations?" Salim's voice came out high, "But they were banned a while back."

"And yet, they have continued to happen." Azlan said, as he watched Salim's shock grow. "In fact, Gedrosia is now being led by a cyborg."

"And it is not me," Mazu added.

Salim crinkled his nose. "Then, who?"

"Idris Aklan," Mazu said.

"Idris has *Transformed?*" Salim sounded even more surprised. "But he's in prison."

"Apparently not," Azlan replied coolly, "He underwent the Transformation and ninety seven percent of him is now all bot, removing every trace of his past. He's Oran – the Chief Scientist here, and quite a ruthless slave of the Syndicate."

Mazu turned to Salim. "Well, he's not quite as ruthless as you think. I think we can get him to come around. After all, I too, am a cyborg."

"But I still can't believe that he has been Transformed." Salim muttered, "especially since he would know what the process can do to you." Then, the professor turned to Mazu. "By the way, what about you? How are you doing after the Transformation?"

"Alive and kicking, that's all I can say. You know, I had nothing to lose. The doctors had given me only a month to live. So, in a way, I have gotten more years by Transforming. I believe Idris was in a similar predicament."

"Well, if there's one person who could beat death, it's you Mazu." Azlan slapped him on the back.

Mazu smiled for a second, then his expression grew grave once again. "But listen, what I and Oran went through is nothing compared to what the Syndicate is doing now."

"What do you mean?" Azlan asked.

Mazu sighed. "You see, new Transformation processes use dynamic DNA coding to ensure synthetic material and biological material can sync. This allows cyborgs to reproduce."

Azlan added. "It also means that cyborgs could soon replace the human race."

Salim was listening with his mouth wide open.

Mazu turned to Azlan. "You're right. But they haven't been successful in creating such cyborgs. In fact, the current process is extremely risky, mind you." Mazu's voice was strangled, almost in anguish as he choked on his own words, "many, if not all, have lost their lives in this process."

"How many people know about this?" Azlan asked.

"Jumander knew of these plans, which is why he was killed." Mazu said.

Salim's eyes enlarged. Where there was confusion, now there was grief, shock and anguish. "You have proof of all this? The Transformations and also... Jumander's involvement?"

Mazu sighed. "We have enough proof that would warrant an investigation into the CHB Syndicate. And about Jumander, well, its complicated." Mazu then turned around and picked up the small cardboard box that was hidden behind him. "This is something for you Salim. Something from Jumander."

Salim stared at them in disbelief, then put the box on the floor and opened it to examine the contents. He saw some photographs, letters and a vintage orblight with a J inscribed on it. He sighed and opened one of the letters that was addressed to himself.

"Dear Salim, if you find this, it means we are no longer here. We know you are already the parent that Jay deserved, but we cannot rest until we end the monster that we started. This was our idea and now, we have blood on our hands. We must see an end to the Syndicate. And we turn to you for help. Above all, you must protect Jay."

Salim stared at the letter and felt that it was cut short. He could tell that the last part was scrobbled, as if they were short on time. Then, as he held onto the box, he noticed small tears streaming down his eyes.

"I know Salim," Mazu bent down and patted his back, "but Jumander knew all along what the Syndicate was planning to do with the Sanctuaries."

"Jumander knew about the Syndicate's plans for Transformations?" Azlan finally reacted. "Never liked the guy."

Mazu turned to Azlan. "Yes, but Jumander was not a murderer. He was our friend. And even if he started what he did, he knew that he had to put an end to it." Then, Mazu turned to Salim. "I think Jay will be happy to know that as well."

Salim let all the information soak in for a moment. The lies and the secrecy, especially from Jumander himself, was deceitful as much as it was sad. Perhaps that is how Jahan felt all along.

After overcoming the initial shock, Salim finally asked, "So what are we to do now?"

Mazu meanwhile took out a piece of folded envelope from his pocket. It was blue, with an insignia.

"What is that?" Azlan asked as he stared at the odd letter.

"For the UR?" said Salim.

Mazu shook his head. "Yes, it is a message that we need to deliver to the UR. It has all the evidence that is pertinent for shutting down Gedrosia, and maybe even the entire Syndicate for the crimes they've committed."

"We?" Salim looked confused. "I don't want to get involved in any of this Gedrosia business anymore. I am only here for Jay.

Mazu grabbed him by the shoulder. "The UR Premier – Moira - has agreed to meet you," then paused, "and you're the only one she will actually listen to."

Salim's cheeks turned a shade of orange at the mention of the name, Moira. Moira Harper was the UR Premier, who had briefly been Salim's sweetheart back when both were newly recruited to work on the CHB mission in Davos, she as a representative from the UR, and Salim as a representative from the Academia de Indus. They had come a long way since then.

Salim shifted uncomfortably. "I don't know, Mazu. It's been a while..." then after a pause, he looked up his brows furrowed. "And what of Jahan? I have to find her and get her home."

"You and Jahan will both leave here safely, and I will make sure of it. All we are asking of you is that you take this letter with you." Mazu looked back at him pleadingly. "Salim, I wouldn't be asking you if I didn't mean it. All of us are under surveillance, and cannot send this in any other way that won't spark suspicion. This letter is the only way the UR can take action on the Syndicate. That's what Jumander would have wanted."

Salim didn't respond. Mazu stepped closer to him and for the first time, spoke in a more sinister tone. "I'm aware you're her guardian, Salim. But I won't conceal this from you: though the girl is safe for now, she won't be for long. Not unless we can bring down the Syndicate."

Salim frowned. "Even if I do agree to your plan, I have a full-time job... I mean the earliest I could go is next Saturday, but the flight to Peking and the vaccinations... it takes a while."

Mazu's face lightened up. "Don't worry about these minor details. We will arrange all that."

Salim inspected the contents of the letter and felt that he didn't really have a choice. It was the right thing to do, and it wasn't much to begin with. "Fine," said Salim. "Now, can I see my god daughter?"

Mazu turned to Azlan, " Can you take Salim to Jay and then, maybe help them get out?"

"Aren't you in charge of the exits and entries?" Azlan asked Mazu.

"I am. But presently, an alert has gone out to block all the main exits. The Landing Dock is entirely inaccessible. The other two routes have a large Jotun presence. The only option out for Salim, Jay and their friends would be an exit through the Makran tunnels. And you are the master of those tunnels."

"So, you're talking about the CAECA-2?" Azlan said.

Mazu nodded.

There was a momentary pause. Azlan's mouth was a little dry. Finally, he coughed. "Okay, it's fine; we can take CAECA-2." Then, with a more pointed tone, he asked.

"Are there other things in this plan you want to fill me in?"

"Glad you've asked," Mazu said as he looked at both of them with a smile. "Follow me gentlemen."

CHAPTER 20

Time to Go

It was late in the evening in Gedrosia, and the light outside was slowly and steadily dimming. Jay was sifting through the books on Azlan's shelves, curiosity brimming inside her. She was slowly discovering what a marvel Gedrosia was and the effort it took in making this underground world habitable. But this concept of Gedrosia apparently existed centuries ago.

Throughout history, mankind had built underground cities, some that were still well preserved even today. But it was only during the twenty-first century that a decision was made to bring this concept back, to exploit underground spaces in what was an already crowded world. She was engrossed in reading about urban underground habitation, including the development of advanced skylights, when Boro nudged at her.

"What's the matter Boro?" Jay asked as she placed the book back in one of the shelves.

Boro cleared his throat. "Jay, I think I have reason to believe that Erol is here." He paused. "In Gedrosia."

"Erol?" Jay's eyes widened as she looked into the bot's eyes. "Here, in Gedrosia?!"

Boro nodded.

"How do you know?"

"Right." Boro quickly turned to his Skinpad. "I just checked my tracking system earlier and discovered Erol's locator pop up a few hours ago. I can't detect him now, but he was definitely here a while back."

"Do you know where could be, now?" Jay asked uncertainly.

Boro's metal lips locked in a purse. "It is difficult to ascertain. The locator disappeared three hours ago and for some reason, I cannot detect him anymore. But I can tell you where I last saw him." Boro then revealed a map with two ticking dots, one that represented them and the other that represented Erol.

Jay examined the map on the Skinpad. From the looks of it, Erol was only five kilometres northeast of their current location.

"He seems close," Jay said as she rubbed her chin. "If only we can find a map to get to him…" Then, her eyes wandered to Azlan's room. She remembered that there was a book that Azlan had been reading when she first saw him. It was supposed to have instructions on how to get out of Gedrosia. That is what she needed.

As she went through the books, she finally came across it: *A Series of Karez Maps Documenting the Ancient Routes for Water Transport.* Excitedly, she grabbed the book from its place, discovering that it was filled with a number of maps and schematics.

"Look, Boro! I found it!" Jay called out to the bot, who stood beside her.

"What did you find?" asked the bot.

"The book that Azlan was reading when I got here. He said this book would help him escape Gedrosia."

"And?"

Jay smiled back. "Well, maybe it can help us as well."

Boro looked at her sceptically, then stretched out his hand. Jay handed the bot the book and watched him quickly sleeve through the pages without so much as a word.

"So?" she asked impatiently, "What does it say?"

Boro didn't respond. Instead, he quietly went about sifting through the book, absorbing its contents. Finally, he muttered, "Quite interesting..."

"What's interesting?" Jay asked impatiently.

Boro finally stopped and turned to her to narrate: "Gedrosia it appears, is surrounded by tunnels that were once ancient water shafts. These shafts, the Makran tunnels, used to deliver water across the Maka province a long time ago. Now, they have been exploited to develop this subterranean world." Boro pointed at the map. "Quite ingenious, don't you think?"

Jay carefully examined the map in the book, furrowing her eyes.

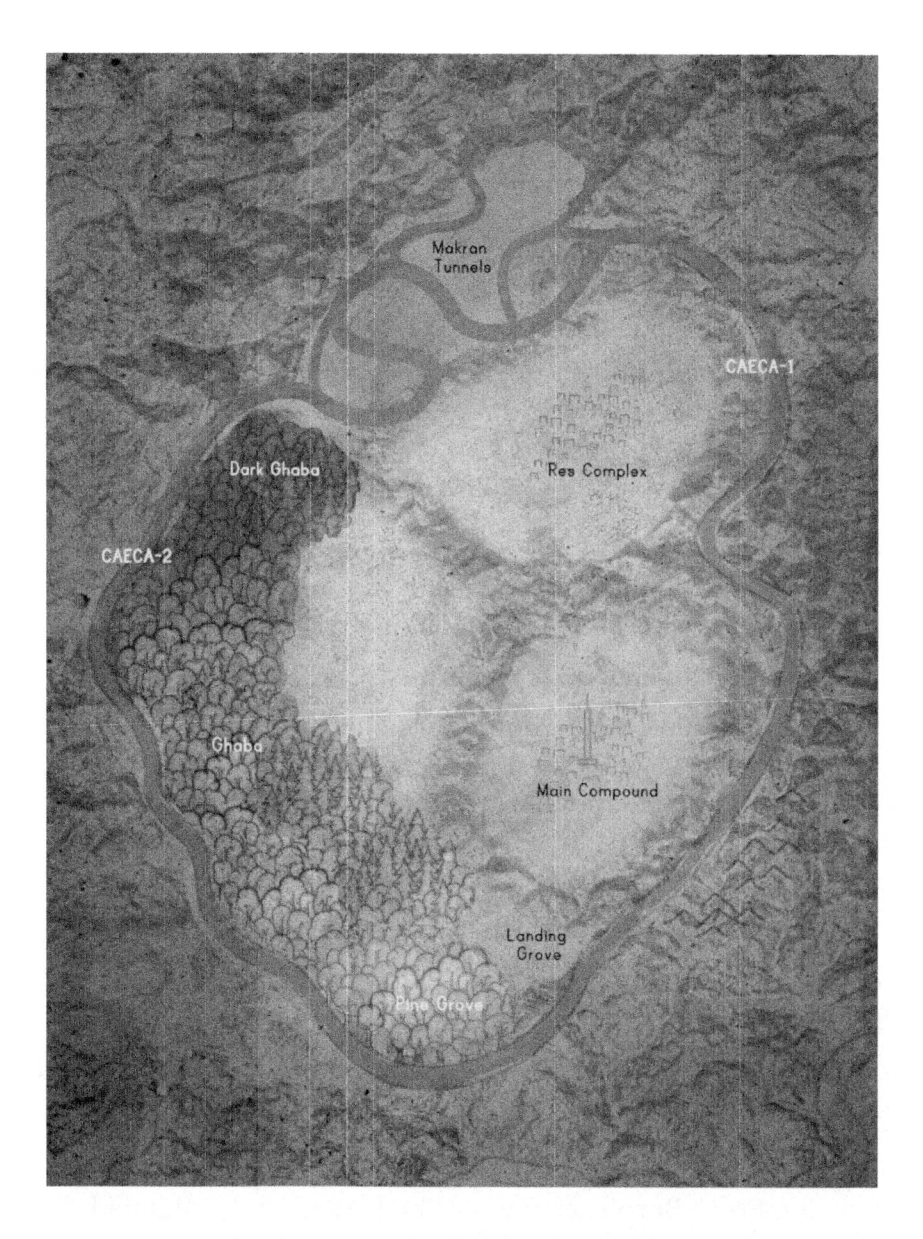

"Do you think these tunnels can help us get to Erol?" Jay asked.

"I don't see why not." Boro then pointed at a tunnel that circled much of the area. "There's a tunnel labeled CAECA-1 which surrounds Gedrosia. I have read through this book carefully and discovered that this particular tunnel opens up in different areas including the Res Complex, the Ghaba and the Main Compound. If we can get to this tunnel from Azlan's home, we could navigate our way to Erol. And even find a way out."

"A way out? So you think these tunnels could lead us back to the surface?" Jay looked at Boro excitedly.

"I think so. If this tunnel is a water shaft, it should also have vertical shafts that should allow us to get back to the surface. This CAECA-1 seems very promising."

"And what is this CAECA-2?" Jay asked as she pointed at another label on the map.

Boro frowned. "You know, I do not know. There is nothing written about this CAECA-2. I think it might be a typo."

"I see. And what about the Jotuns?"

Boro looked prepared for this question. "Well, you might remember Azlan saying that the only places under surveillance are those under skylight. These Makran tunnels do not have a skylight. They appear to be outside of Gedrosia altogether so they might not be under the watch of any Jotuns."

Jay smiled. "Well then, what are we waiting for?"

Boro hesitated. "Azlan did tell us to wait for him here. Perhaps we can head out once he is back."

Before Jay could protest, a beep came from Boro's Skinpad, making her startle.

"What is it?" Jay asked.

"It's Erol." Boro exclaimed as he looked at the Skinpad. "His locator has popped up again." A short pause. "He is very close to us."

"That settles it, Boro." Jay said. "He's here and he's close. We should get to him before the Jotuns do."

Boro stared at her for a second, then looked at the Skinpad. There was a moment of lull before he sighed. "Okay. I will work on a tomography program to help us on the way."

"A tomo-what?"

Boro was clicking away at his Skinpad. "Just a program that will help me map this entire place out."

"Okay...." Jay looked confused. "Do what you must."

"Just give me a second." With that, Boro quickly glanced over the books in Azlan's shelves, and grabbed some, stuffing them in Jay's bag.

Then, before they finally left, Jay left a note for Azlan informing him that they were on their way out of Gedrosia.

※※※

Jay followed Boro out of the main tunnel Azlan had left from. It was low and narrow requiring both of them to crouch a little. The walls were smooth and near perfect shape. One would suppose that it was a manmade tunnel, expect for the fact that it didn't extend in a straight line. Instead, it meandered left and right, declining and ascending.

"This explains it." Boro muttered. "You see, these were water shafts before which explains why they are so smooth – but they go up and down like water."

"Ah!"

Right, left, left, right, they went, following the twists in the tunnel, which seemed to be broadening. Finally, the tunnel opened up into a majestic cavern.

Both of them halted.

They were standing at the edge of a shallow bowl-shaped basin that formed the floor of the cave. Above them, a darker obsidian rock filled the sky, arching down in the middle.

Luminescent rocks lined the cavity and their reflections by the obsidian rock above them lit up the entire cavern in a magical purple ember. Lining the basin were smaller passages going out in all directions.

"Woah, what is this place?" Jay asked as she walked towards the centre of the large basin.

"It looks like a cistern," Boro looked at the Skinpad, and began clicking away.

"What are you doing?" Jay asked, as she looked down at what Boro was coding.

"This is the program I was mentioning earlier," Boro answered as he clicked a few buttons. "My emitter can send out signals of different wavelengths and my processor can determine material and thickness of the walls, using the time of travel."

"Ah…" Jay nodded while she gave this a thought. "But what about reflections and …"

Boro smiled, almost expecting the question. "Reflections are exactly what will help me. I'll be able to assess which of these passages have thinner walls that we can break out of to get back to the skylight-Gedrosia."

"I see." Jay mumbled, still uncertain about the process. "Well then, let's have a go at it."

Boro nodded firmly, then shut his eyes as a long baton appeared from the middle of his metal scalp, a red light on top blinking. Finally, the beeping ended, and the bot opened his eyes, his orbitals a red hue. "Now, wait till you see this." Boro was quick to pull up a holographic projection, which looked like a spiderweb of blue lines.

Jay examined it closely. It was a blurry schematic of the entire subterranean world with varying thickness of walls. The walls were snake-like, spiralling round and round, interconnected barriers running length on length. Below this web of interconnected tunnels was a hollow section, with shadows of structures, their thickness and material unclear though. Two red dots blinked within the tunnels, while a green dot flickered at the centre of the map, within a hollow section.

Boro pointed at the green dot. "This green dot is in Gedrosia under skylight, the hollow section. Which part of Gedrosia, I am not sure. These two red dots show our location, Jay," Boro explained, as his finger traced the schematic. "As you can see, we are within the Makran tunnels outside of 'hollow' Gedrosia altogether."

Jay nodded her head, her eyes falling on the green blinking dot at the centre of the map. "That's Erol?"

"Yes."

"It looks like he's quite close to these tunnels. Do you know how we could get to him?"

"I can try." Boro said, as he looked at the Skinpad once more, then walked across the basin into one of the many passages that connected to the basin. It was apparently narrower than the others, its light dimmer and walls, obsidian. "Let's take this way."

They continued along the slender passage, which grew ever narrower with distance. Jay could feel the weight of the rock around her pressing down. She tried to take deep breaths but felt like she was choking.

"Boro, let's go back. This doesn't look like it will lead us out." Jay choked on the words as she felt a wave of nausea hit her. "Also, I can't breathe."

"I promise it will open up soon," Boro said. "We need to keep going."

But Jay continued to feel unwell. "I don't think I'm feeling so good," the girl paused, looking ahead at the long, narrow tunnel, "I think I want to go back."

By now, the girl had no desire to go any further into the narrow, darkened passage, one that felt like it may collapse on her forever. Then again, what was she thinking. She was searching for the 'hidden caves' of Gedrosia. No wonder skylights and holograms were needed to make the subterranean liveable.

"Just another hundred meters." Boro grabbed her.

Fortunately for Jay, the tunnel did get brighter, the air fresher. They were in an older-looking tunnel, wider and longer than the others. Gypsum coated the walls, giving it that peculiar pink shine, and fluorescent rocks, larger than the ones they had seen before, lined the floor.

"This is CAECA-1," Boro said.

"I can't believe we found it." Jay felt a huge surge of relief. "Do we continue ahead?"

Boro turned to his Skinpad, then nodded. After a hundred meters or so, they arrived at a three-way bend.

"Now, which way?" she asked.

Boro looked left and right, peering down the tunnels. Finally, with a swift movement, he grabbed Jay's hand, leading her to the right. The tunnel continued to go in the same direction, until it began to curve back like a U-turn. Jay gave Boro a concerned look, but the bot kept prodding on, pointing straight ahead. Up ahead, Jay saw a sharp bend. Onwards they went, rounding the bend, until they arrived at a blank stone wall.

"What!" Jay stomped her foot. It was a dead end. She turned to Boro, frown lines on her face. "We are stuck."

Meanwhile, Boro brushed past her gently, and began examining the wall. He noticed a stone dais on the floor right in front of the wall. The bot stepped on the dais expecting it to move, but nothing happened. He began to feel along the stones, moving his hands over the surface almost as if he knew what he was looking for.

"There!" he exclaimed after less than one minute, the smile on his face barely perceptible in the dim light. He pushed hard on one of the stones, which caused the ground to shake and the dais to slide back. This sliding caused one of the adjacent stone slabs to rotate, swerving Jay onto the other side of the dead-end wall.

Jay quickly stepped off the rotating stone slab and found herself at another three-way junction, with a tunnel straight in front of her, and two tunnels branching in opposite directions, one to the left and the other to the right. Behind her was the wall that separated her from Boro.

"Boro, can you hear me?" she asked, putting her ears back to the wall.

"Yes, where are you?"

"I think I'm behind you, behind this wall. Perhaps you can try to get on the dais as well and get around to this side."

"But there is no dais..."

Jay didn't hear the entire sentence. Her ears were on high alert. Alarmed, she looked around and realized that someone or something was close by. The sound of metal thudding was audible and becoming louder and louder.

And then, she knew that this was it. The Jotuns had found her.

***

Jay stared at the tunnel ahead of her, listening to her death rushing to greet her. The thumping of the metal footsteps could not be mistaken. Jotuns were near, their metal armour echoing across the walls. A wave of panic hit her. This was it. She was trapped and the Jotuns would soon have her. Perhaps, this was the same way her parents were trapped. The hopelessness of the situation left her with a dull relief: she no longer needed to run. But then, with some will of hers, she snapped out of it. It wasn't like Jahan Jumander to give up like this.

In no mood to disappear just yet, Jay closed her eyes and tried to listen to where the sound was coming from. She guessed it to be somewhere to her northwest. Quickly, she swerved into the tunnel going right, while throwing the torch behind her, in the tunnel that went left. The bots seemed closer now: Jay knew that she was a hair's breadth away from the bots seeing her turn and had just narrowly evaded the inevitable beam of their lasgun which would have incinerated her in minutes.

Quickly but silently, she ran ahead on tiptoes, arriving at another three-way fork. With a quick decision and prayer, she turned right, tumbling into a small alcove. The metal footsteps grew more silent, the sounds further away, as the bots appeared to have followed the torch onto the other side. Jay sighed before she collapsed onto the wall of the tunnel, panting from this close encounter with the bots. After a few moments, she closed her eyes, overcome by the relief that only such a close brush with mortality could bring.

But an instant later, Jay flailed her arms helplessly, the walls of the tunnel collapsing behind her. She slipped back, further down, lower and lower, perhaps two or three levels below, into a dark room. She looked up and saw the slight light from the tunnel she fell through.

For a moment, Jay just sat there on the rubble, closing her eyes to allow a momentary surge of claustrophobic panic to pass. This peace was short-lived though. A sudden fear gripped her as she heard approaching rodents. She sat bolt upright, groping around in the inky darkness, trying to climb her way back up.

But there was nothing to hold on to or to climb back. The opening was too far up.

Meanwhile, the rodents drew nearer, their sounds growing. Panic-stricken and in the dark, Jay began searching for rocks or something hard to hurl at the rodents. She only found debris. As the tiny footsteps began to multiply, Jay began kicking with her hands and feet in the dark open space. Suddenly, her feet met some object. Revolted, she began to kick even more furiously. Small squeals accompanied each strike as her shoes found their furry targets. Finally, the squeals began to die down.

Still shaking with revulsion and fear, Jay tried to calm herself and devise a way out of her predicament. She couldn't waste her energy. She searched around for a rock to climb on to and get through the wall. Despite these efforts, she saw no escape. The wall was too steep and too high to climb. She began to use her feet to guide her around the room, trying to see if there was a hole that the rodents may have come from.

As she felt her way around the wall, she touched something clammy like metal. For a second, she wondered if it might be some bot part.

It was an arm. Jay was panicking but took deep breaths. Meanwhile, another metal arm gripped her from behind. Before she could scream, the arm came over her mouth as someone whispered in her ears.

"Shh. It's Boro."

※※※

"You won't believe what I saw."

Stepping over the rocks littered across the floor, Jay followed Boro into the approximate centre of the pit she had fallen into. There, Boro focused his eyelights to the ceiling. Jay looked up. About twelve feet above her and all around the pit were at least four or five tunnels, including the one she had fallen from. All of these tunnels terminated into this pit, probably from different locations. Boro lifted himself through one of the tunnels before lifting Jay up.

Up ahead, Boro lit up the alcove they were in. It was brick walled, suggesting it was manmade.

"Look at this," said the bot as he pointed at the set of paw prints on the walls. Jay leaned in closer, touching them and realizing they were all red and wet.

"Boro, is this…?" Without finishing the sentence, she sniffed her soaked hands. Then, she moved her hand to Boro, who performed a retinal scan on the red liquid.

"It is indeed blood. Mammalian. And it is fresh," Boro affirmed. "Perhaps we should get out of here."

Jay felt sick to the stomach, until a thought flashed. "What if this blood might lead us to some kind of evidence?"

"What evidence? This is blood."

"But why is there blood on the tunnels? It's worth investigating further into. It might lead us to some answers."

Boro glared at her. "It will *only* lead us to trouble," then nudged her. "Follow me."

Jay nodded, then wiped away the blood on her clothes. They trudged on, walking faster and realizing that the tunnel was opening up. Up ahead, they saw a faint light drawing them in further. The tunnel opened into a chamber with another tunnel entrance to the right. Just as Jay was running over to the entrance tunnel, Boro grabbed her arm. His expression grew solemn as he signalled her with his fingers to stay quiet. In the ensuing silence and stillness, both of them heard the panting sound of a creature. Adding to Jay's shock, there lay on the floor of this pit, multiple skeletal remains.

But these were no ordinary skeletons. Metal poked out from the skeletal remains, replacing bone in some sections. Where there was a socket, was instead a metal ball. Jay swallowed, her heart racing as she studied the human-robot skeletons. And right at the corner was a silhouette of something humanlike lying on the floor in the left-hand corner. The bot walked towards the shadow, Jay timidly following behind.

It was a human with bot legs and arms, coiled up in a foetal position. Its face was discernibly human, and it was staring wildly at the two of them in a defensive position. Boro edged towards the creature, but almost in alarm, with a turn of the torso, the human's chest immediately transformed into a metallic plate.

Boro retreated as he saw this metamorphosis, but Jay leaned in further to examine the creature. "Wait a moment, it seems like it's injured!" She pointed at the blood on the shoulder. Closer now, the girl noticed that the chest had stopped moving.

"Is he...dead?" Jay stuttered, as she bent down to touch its flesh-like chassis. Immediately, the thing twitched a bit, its metal pieces becoming fleshy, until it became limp again.

"Jay, this is a...cyborg," Boro said. "It could be dangerous."

"He's injured..." Jay began to look around his shoulder to find the source of the blood. Just as soon as she touched the wounded shoulder, the thing transformed again, this time entirely into an ape-like animal. In a short instance, the animal grabbed Jay's legs, dragging her towards it.

"Let go of me!" Jay yelled as she pulled away from the cyborg.

The cyborg almost helplessly held his hands in a prayer. "Please help me."

"Who are you?" Boro asked as he stepped between the cyborg and Jay. "And what is this place?"

"You both should not be here. If he finds out, he will kill you." The cyborg spoke.

"Who will found out, who will kill us?" Jay asked with urgency. "And what is this place?"

"It's where they dispose the bodies of those that failed Transformation."

"Transformation? As in..." Jay was cut off by Boro who was tugging at her arm. "We need to go, Jay. Now!"

Jay could hear the muffled sounds of footsteps somewhere in the tunnels.

"Boro, wait. Record this." She looked at the tunnel, gulped as she heard the footsteps get louder, then turned to the cyborg.

"I can help you if you can help me. Tell me how we can put an end to these Transformations?"

The cyborg stared at her quietly. Then, after a while, he looked down to himself and pushed his hand through his chest, through flesh and wiring, to grab a small chip and pull it apart from his body. As soon as he did, his head and arms flailed in lifelessness.

Jay nudged the shoulders, but the cyborg didn't respond. She let out a quiet wail. Meanwhile, Boro stepped forward and gently opened the cyborg's closed fist.

There was a chip.

"He must have wanted us to have this." Boro said.

"I think it might be all the evidence we need." Jay turned to him, then back at the cyborg. "He sacrificed himself."

The silence was short-lived as both Jay and Boro could hear the fast approaching Jotuns.

"Let's go." Boro said.

"Okay..." Jay hesitated. "So where do we..."

Before Jay could finish, Boro grabbed her hand. "Follow me."

Jay followed him unquestioningly into the tunnel, her mind still on what the cyborg had done. A few steps afterwards, Boro reduced his pace.

"Quiet," Boro hissed as he held up his fingers for silence. Jay slowed down, trying to make out the faint sound. Then, they both heard it. The low, rhythmic ring of metal on rock, followed by hissed voices somewhere behind the walls of the tunnel.

".... Overground...escape."

Boro and Jay exchanged a quick glance. Quietly, Jay placed her ears onto the wall to listen carefully.

"...Intruders...complex..."

"...shut...exit..."

Quickly, Jay began to follow the Jotuns down the tunnel. "This way," she instructed Boro, as she followed the sounds.

"*Why* are we *following* them?" Boro whispered. "We need to get *away* from them."

Jay stared at him. "I think they are planning to block the exits. If we want to get out of here, we need to know what exits they are blocking, so that we don't end up in a trap." She paused. "We need to be one step ahead of them."

Boro looked at her with a cold expression. "Fine! But I lead!"

Jay gave him a lopsided grin, as he brushed past her and continued down the tunnel trailing the Jotuns, yet keeping to the sides of the darkened passages. The voices of the Jotuns drew closer, echoing eerily in the dark passages. Jay followed Boro, slowly tiptoeing and arriving at a fork in the tunnel.

From their vantage point, they could spot the two Jotuns turning left and disappearing into another branching tunnel. They seemed to be oblivious to the fact that Jay and Boro were behind them.

Cautiously, Jay and Boro followed them, watching for any movement along the passages, then darting from tunnel to tunnel. A few times, the Jotuns looked back but missed them both.

Finally, the Jotuns stopped abruptly at a three-end fork facing a dead end. Immediately, Jay and Boro froze in their places, hoping the Jotuns wouldn't turn around, as they slowly tiptoed back to the bend in the tunnel, and hid behind it, peaking at the Jotuns.

They watched the Jotuns knock on the wall in front of them. This was followed by a faint thud coming from the dead-end wall.

Then, bright morning light came through from the shaft. Finally, the entire door opened to reveal the forest resplendent in daylight. A very heavily uniformed Jotun, almost military-ish, stood outside in the doorway.

Jay squinted and saw the military Jotun open a bag to reveal a small arsenal of ray guns and explosives, as he addressed the other Jotuns. "Block the exits and if you see anyone, don't hesitate. We have orders." Then, after handing them the weapons, the military Jotun left, closing the door behind them. The two Jotuns then turned to the right of the fork, carrying the arsenal with them.

Meanwhile, Jay and Boro remained hidden behind the tunnel and waited for a while as the sound of the Jotuns got further away.

"They're going to block the exits," Jay spoke once the sound of the footstep's had disappeared altogether. "How'll we get out?"

"Let's leave that for later. Right now, we need to get to Erol who is just outside that door." Boro pointed up ahead.

Jay's eyes widened. "How do you know?"

Boro turned to his Skinpad. "Up ahead is the forest. And Erol's ticker is right there."

Jay gulped. "But the Jotuns?"

"I know, which is why we need to get to him first. He is in danger."

"Okay," Jay sighed. "You're right."

They waited to make sure no one was near. When the coast seemed clear, they made their way down the tunnel to the dead-end door. Boro took the lead and leaned his ear on the door to see if he could hear anything.

"There is no one."

The bot slowly opened the door and peeked outside into the open. Then, turned back. "All clear."

They slid through the wall, emerging out of a hill and into the forest. It was a part of the forest they were unfamiliar with. Jay looked around in the open, invigorated with a strange self-confidence that had possessed her.

"Erol is close." Boro remarked, as he projected the holomap in front of them. "In fact, he should be right around the corner."

Jay examined the map and saw the green dot that represented Erol ticking and nearing the two red dots.

"It seems he has found us!" Boro exclaimed. The green ticking dot was moving on the screen, coming closer. But abruptly—it stopped.

"What's wrong?" Jay asked.

Before Boro could answer, he jerked around. There was a snapping sound like somebody stepping on a branch. Then, another one, closer this time. They both looked behind the forest but there was no one there. Then, as they turned back around, in a sudden flurry of activity, branches parted all around them and two Jotuns burst through, followed by a human in his lab coats.

One of the Jotuns seized Boro from behind while the other grabbed Jay. In that instant, both of them dodged their grasp and began to run at full speed. But their freedom was short-lived. A beam of light shot the ground in front of Jay, barely missing her.

"What the..." she looked around and another beam hit the ground causing her to fall sideways and roll to the ground.

"Jay, find cover!" Boro yelled from afar. Still on the ground, Jay lifted herself only to find a vaguely familiar bot appear from the forest, pointing its lasgun at her. It was a bulbous looking bot, similar to the one she had seen earlier with Boro and Erol in the Makran desert.

The bulbous bot glared at her, his eyes glowing a fierce red. Behind him, the two Jotuns turned to face her as one, thumping their feet in anticipation.

"Wait," Jay yelled as she tried to get up, her hands up in the air. "Don't shoot. We didn't do anything."

"We know who you are." A bearded man donning a white lab coat came up from behind the Jotuns. "Jay Jumander."

Boro came up from behind, unconsciously closing his hands into fists ready to attack, but before he could make another move, the man was already pointing a lasgun at Jay.

"I can kill you now – or if you prefer, you can cooperate with me and I can take you to Oran."

Jay gulped and slowly got up. "What do you want from us?"

"Nothing my dear. I'm afraid this is something you can't get out of. Now, follow me." The man was already walking away while the bulbous bot and Jotuns stood around them, pointing their guns.

"Do I have to repeat myself?" the man yelled. "Follow me."

Without uttering another word, Jay and Boro slowly got up, and proceeded to follow the man. They were taken to the edge of the forest, where a Landstorm was waiting for them. Immediately, the two Jotuns shackled Jay and Boro with metal handcuffs.

"Get in." The man ordered. Boro and Jay complied as the tip of the lasguns nudged them from the back.

"You both," the man gestured the Jotuns, "Stay behind for the other intruders."

Jay knew who he was talking about. Erol was the intruder, and now in danger because of her. This time around, there was no escape; she realized this was the end of her journey.

CHAPTER 21

Hacking the system

"**A**re you sure it's your bot?"

"Yeah, I'm sure," said Erol. "I programmed that GPS signal into him myself."

Erol and Faruk were making their way out of the shack and into the Dark Ghaba, following the signal that Boro had sent. They knew it was coming from somewhere close to the Dark Ghaba, but they weren't so sure where.

"The signal says he's close."

"You better be right because we were given strict orders to stay inside."

Erol grinned and followed his GPS into the winding path that took them from the Dark Ghaba and into the Gedrosian forest that was lit up by the skylight. They continued walking through the forest, careful to stay under the canopy of the trees, knowing that the skylight was also a surveillance tool. After walking for at least a mile, they came across a muddy portion of the forest surrounded by gnarly trees and odd rock outcrops. Erol bent down and inspected the location. There were damp grooves near the trees. Someone—or something—had recently been there.

Faruk eased himself down on one of the large roots of the trees that was protruding out of the ground. "This is the first time I'm getting to explore a real forest."

"Oh yeah?" Erol asked but was visibly more concerned by the grooves.

"Yeah. Never seen something as lush as this place. I'm glad I came."

"Me too," said Erol. But no sooner had he decided to sit beside Faruk on the root, they both heard distant muffled sounds and then a scream.

"What was that?" Faruk asked, looking around the forest.

"Shhh," said Erol as he pulled Faruk down as they took refuge behind a large root. "Get down."

Hunkered behind the gnarly root of the tree, the two could hear the sound of snapping sticks coming from a dense section in the forest. Erol craned his neck, squinting his eyes and finally saw two figures emerge from a thicket of trees. Boro and Jay.

"Ja-" but before Erol could call out to them, Faruk grabbed him from behind. "Shhh... they're being taken in," he paused, "as prisoners."

Erol stared at Faruk, then slowly turned his gaze back at the sight of his friends. Faruk was right. From behind Jay and Boro emerged two armoured bots who were nudging them both forward. Right beside the bots was a human clad in a white coat.

"They must be in danger," Erol whispered, concern in his voice. Slowly, he moved closer, making sure at each step that his body was well hidden behind the trees and their trunks.

"Where are they taking them?" Erol crouched behind a large bush and continued to follow them with his gaze. They continued through an opening in the forest, then entered another thicket of trees, until they finally disappeared altogether into the jungle, as if they had been swallowed whole.

The ruffling sounds faded away soon after the sight, and after a while of silence, Erol started to get up from his crouched position, "We have to do something or else we'll lose them."

"Shh..." Faruk grabbed him, pulling him back behind the bush. "We aren't alone." The boy pointed back at the same thicket opening, and saw the two Jotuns return, leaving behind the sound of an ignition turning.

"Looks like those bots are staying back for more prisoners," Erol said, a slow grin forming on his face.

"Why are you grinning?" Faruk seemed furious. "Those bots are after us, that's what!"

"But they can help us find Jay and Boro," Erol whispered, as he snuck closer to the bots, scurrying from bush to bush. Faruk stared at Erol wide-eyed, convinced there was something wrong with him.

Erol turned to explain. "I know this sounds crazy but if we can disengage them, then we can reprogram and use them."

"Are you crazy? I'm not getting myself killed."

"Listen, that's the only way we can get to Jay. If we reprogram them, we can even pretend to be their prisoners and they can lead us straight to Jay and Boro."

"Sorry man. She's not my girlfriend. I am not putting my neck on the line for this."

Erol was red. "She's not my girlfriend, aw'right? But she *is* my friend and she'd do the same for me."

"What a fool," Faruk muttered under his breath. "And how do you plan to disengage and reprogram those bots?"

"Well, the disengaging part's easy." Erol gave him a smug grin. "I know a thing or two about bots. They have a weak spot – their nape. A hit can result in stunning for thirty seconds. In those thirty seconds, I need to access their ROS. You know the Robot Operating System. Then, they are fully disengaged."

"Thirty seconds is cutting too close and those don't look like ordinary bots." Faruk looked worried.

"I know. But I'm willing to take my chances. Now, tell me, you are the hacker. Can you hack into the operating system? We can then work on re-programming it?"

Faruk's lip pursed as he gave it some thought, then they finally curved into a smile. He coyly combed his hair with his fingers and took out the hackpad from his pocket, "Well, I did win a hacking Olympiad. So, I am sure I can figure it out."

***

"Quickly now." Erol was panting as he lifted the chassis of the large bot who was lying stunned on the floor.

"They're heavy." Faruk's hands were shaking.

As soon as the two bots were stunned, Erol quickly opened the shaft in the nape of one of the bot's neck. It revealed a battery slot next to a multitude of coloured wires. Quickly, he took out a battery from his pocket. Faruk gave him an odd look.

"I always carry spare batteries. Never attempt to reprogram a bot without replacing the batteries with a fresh set." Then, as Erol replaced the batteries on the other bot, he explained, "If internal power cuts out in the middle of reprogramming and there's no backup power, there's a chance that the micro-controller will get its fuses misconfigured and will become unresponsive."

Faruk nodded. "And the ROS?"

Erol examined the chest of the bot, searching for a seam line. "No ROS here. You search the other one for any seam line."

Faruk quickly searched the other bot for seams. "What if they have a remote ROS. What if it's not on them?"

But Erol ignored him and continued to search the body for any seam line, taking all the fabric off its large, metal body.

"Quick. Look behind the thigh," Erol ordered Faruk. "The seams are likely to be around joints."

And there was a seam.

They both saw it on each of the bots. On the right thigh, just along the entire hamstring, perfectly concealed as a muscle. Erol manoeuvred around the seam, making shapes with his fingers and just seconds before the bots would be online, a holographic console showed up. Erol clicked on the console.

"Voila. We have access to ROS."

Just as the other bot made a loud twitch, Erol jumped onto him and repeated the pattern on his thigh. The console appeared and Erol clicked on it, shutting the bot, just in time.

"Now what?" Faruk asked as he watched Erol write commands on the holographic console.

"I can't seem to get through their firewall," Erol sounded worried, "Can you give me a hand?"

"What do you need me to do?"

"See if you can get through the firewall and access their core program."

Faruk immediately took over writing commands in a language that Erol didn't even know existed. As he worked quickly writing up code almost in real time after new prompts showed up, a bead of sweat went down his forehead. After some few moments of utter stress, a sigh followed.

"All yours," Faruk said.

Erol reprogrammed the bots by changing a small aspect of their main function. They were answerable no longer to an 01 – but to Erol. They performed their hacks on both the bots, rebooted them and waited.

Finally, there was a twitch from one of the bots. Then, another one from the other bot. After a few more of twitches, Erol and Faruk moved back and watched both the bots get up.

Erol had his breath held. Then, one of them spoke, "Hello, J189 at your service, Erol."

"J293 at yours, Erol."

Faruk and Erol looked at one another and smiled.

"J189, J293, you both will be reporting to me, Erol, and Faruk, here, from now on. Do you concur?"

"Affirmative."

"Now, follow us. We need your help in getting into the location that the girl, Jay Jumander, and her accompanying bot will be taken to by the scientist."

The two bots exchanged glances, then nodded back. "Affirmative, Erol and Faruk."

CHAPTER 22

Where is Jay?

Men are certainly creatures of few words, because once they had agreed on their new roles, they operated like clockwork. Leaving the small chamber outfitted with orbs, flares, and WaterMakers, courtesy of Mazu, the trio made their way through the Makran tunnels to head to Azlan's home and retrieve Jay and Boro.

"You *chose* to live here?" Salim turned to Azlan as they walked through the tunnels. "Doesn't it get a bit gloomy to be in these tunnels with no sunlight?"

"Well, there is no sunlight *anywhere* in Gedrosia!" Azlan remarked as they tread through one of the connecting tunnels that led up to the door to his home. "There is only a fake skylight."

"But surely, it's better than this?" asked Salim, still troubled by the thought of living in tunnels.

Azlan glared at him. "Salim, that skylight is like the Syndicate hovering over you, monitoring all your activities. I'd rather choose darkness over being watched anytime. So no, the skylight is not better than these tunnels."

"I see," said Salim quietly. He decided not to probe further but made a mental note never to choose to work anywhere underground, period.

The trio finally arrived at a bowl-shaped basin, with multiple passages emerging from it. Salim quietly followed the two into one of many tunnels connecting to the basin. From there, they all had to duck as they made their way down the tunnel. Continuing along the tunnel, they finally arrived at a large door.

"Home, voila!" Azlan said as he grinned back at them and then opened the door.

"Jay, it's just me." He let out, "I'm back. And guess who else is with me?" Azlan bellowed as he walked around the main chamber and then into his room.

But there was no sign of Jay or Boro.

"Jay!" Salim yelled, but it was clear that there was no one home.

Mazu turned to Azlan, "What is the meaning of this, Azlan? You said she was safe in your home?"

Salim turned around and grabbed Azlan's collar. "You tell me where she is right now!"

"I promise, she was here!" Azlan cried out in defence. "She was here, safe. I left her here, I swear." He turned to Mazu, "And no one knows that she was here."

"Salim, let him go," Mazu finally said as he calmly walked towards the alter in front of the kitchen counter and picked up a piece of paper. "A message."

"What does it say?" Salim cried out aloud.

Mazu read out the contents of the letter quietly, then handed it to Salim. "Jay's gone to find a friend. Said that they detected him and will be back soon."

"What does she mean?" Azlan said, as he grabbed the letter from him. "What friends?"

Salim was panicking internally but tried to keep calm. "She's going to try to go to the shack. To meet Erol, one of the boys who came with me." In his panic, he realized he was sweating profusely and pacing through the room.

"You brought more children underground?!" yelled Azlan, "Are you crazy?"

"Salim, don't worry," Mazu stopped him from pacing. "I will return to the Main Compound and access the skylight surveillance. We will find her in no time."

"So will the Jotuns," said Azlan.

Mazu glared at Azlan. "I have a way to distract them – and Oran. Leave that to me. Salim, you go back to the shack and see if she is there. Search in the Dark Ghaba."

He paused. "And Azlan. You stay here in case she returns. I will send you both a message if I see her anywhere and get her back to you guys."

"Ok," Salim said. "And what if she is lost in the tunnels?"

"Well, then she's safe at least from the Jotuns." Mazu said. "We can search for her in the tunnels once we know for sure she isn't in Gedrosia or the shack anymore. Plan?"

Salim shook his head furiously, though seemed lost. "Okay. Yes. Alright."

Mazu turned to Azlan, whispering, "If anything happens, don't tell Salim. He will needlessly panic. And be on the lookout for Jay."

CHAPTER 23

Captured

Handcuffed, Jay was floating in the pod, her vision hazy from the chemicals in her body. The windows were open, but she closed her eyes, queasy from the constant pitching holographic displays and the pod bumping up and down. For a second, she prayed this was just a bad dream that she'd wake up from.

Very soon, she became attentive as the pod passed by the gates of the Main Compound. The pod pulled over in front of the GM Tower overhead, flashing white and black. An armoured Jotun approached their pod and leaped in front of them, pointing one of the rifle-looking weapons at Jay. *This was it,* Jay thought.

"Hands over your heads!" The Jotun barked at them. Both of them quickly raised their hands until more orders were sounded.

"Take them to Oran," ordered the human. The Jotun nodded, then unslung his weapon.

"Follow me and keep your hands up."

Nervously, with her hands on her head, Jay finally piped up, "Listen, I didn't do anything. I just came—"

"Silence. You can save this all for when you see the Manager later."

Jay and Boro were directed inside and led down some service elevators through the GM tower. A door opened into a very dim looking part of the tower, with opaque rooms lining the aisles.

Boro and Jay were ushered forward by the nudge of the Jotun's weapon. Finally, one door opened, and they were pushed gently but firmly into what was obviously a cell. The door closed with an ominous thud.

Jay looked around, taking stock of her surroundings. It was a small cell with a tiny bunk. Nothing else. A security camera was mounted in one corner, not even discreetly hidden.

"What now?" Jay asked, as she flopped on the lower bunk, "We're doomed."

"I am thinking, Jay," Boro answered, as he walked over to the security camera giving it a long, hard stare. Then, he began pacing back and forth in the room, and although it appeared unproductive, Jay knew it was the only thing that wouldn't spark suspicion.

Hours passed as Jay sat there waiting and wondering how to escape while Boro continued his pacing. In that process, she had drifted to sleep, then gotten up and drifted to sleep again, haunted by thoughts until finally Boro woke her up.

"Time to go," he said as he stood over her like a sentinel.

She got up, groggy and noticed that the door was open. A human was standing at the door, alone, without any bots or Jotuns guarding him. The man looked unarmed as he motioned the prisoners slightly with his hand. "This way. You can see Oran now." His voice sounded sympathetic.

Jay and Boro followed him out and were led through the tower, corridor after corridor, elevator after elevator, until they passed through a glass door labelled **OVERGROUNDERS**. The man led them through the hallway and into another glass door to enter a room that looked much more sterile, like a hospital room. At the centre of the room was what looked like an x-ray machine, or perhaps a lie detector! It looked like an interrogation chamber.

Before they knew what was happening and before they could protest, the man handcuffed them and strapped them onto chairs. Before they knew it, Jay was injected with some drug and Boro was switched off.

"I'm sorry to have to do this," he said, before he left them in the cold, empty and sinister room.

* * *

A strange voice spoke in Jay's head as she lay drugged in a sterile-looking room.

"Shall I kill the girl?" The voice didn't sound human. It had an alien quality in its vibration that set even Jay's dreaming mind bristling.

In response to the question, another disembodied voice answered, "No. That will serve no purpose." The voice seemed more human than the first, lacking the uncanny alien quality, but it still sounded merciless.

Slowly, Jay opened her eyes. These voices were likely all in her head, since there was no one around except for one bot. Oran. And this time, the bot looked much stronger than before.

Was Oran speaking to himself? Jay wondered. Then, she looked around and saw Boro strapped onto a chair. He appeared to be switched off, his systems down and head tilted back.

"Why have you come here, Jay?"

Suddenly, the girl's nerves crawled again at the non-human strangeness of Oran's voice. The bot was standing right over her.

"Why did you really come to Gedrosia?" Oran repeated with a tone of insistence that was impossible to reject. Invigorated by anger, Jay found herself struggling to free herself from the straps.

"You can't get out of these straps," he said calmly. "They only become tauter if you struggle harder."

Jay sank back onto the seat hopelessly.

"I know who your father was Jay, and I know he was trying to reveal the Syndicate's plans," Oran spoke as he walked around the room. "Plans that he had no business meddling in."

Jay looked at the bot coldly.

"Tell me what you know, Jay." Oran said.

"I told you already," Jay said loudly. "I don't know what you are talking about."

"You're not making this any easier, Jay," Oran said. This time, his voice had an uncanny echo. "Tell me what you know about the Syndicate!"

"I told you I don't know anything!" Jay said in a flustered tone.

"Well, then," Oran stood in front of her, licking his lips. "I will let you live, my child if you reveal the names of those who were Jumander's friends, the ones who helped you escape from the Compound." Oran looked at her with disdain.

"What are you talking about?" Jay said.

"Ah... don't be cheeky with me." Oran gave her an evil smile.

"I know you won't let me go or let me live, so why would I bother to tell you anything. You don't believe me when I tell the truth anyways." Jay sounded a bit delirious.

Oran looked at her flatly, then got up from his seat and began to pace in the office as if he were giving a sermon. "Do you know what was special about these ancient places like Agartha or Gedrosia?"

Jay frowned. Why did this bot love giving such grand speeches? Then again, maybe she could buy herself some time with this and try to get out of this situation.

"Uh, that they were all underground civilizations?"

"No, Jay. Agartha and Gedrosia were civilizations of a much superior race," Oran's voice assumed an air of superiority almost as he gestured to the laboratory around him. Then, he waved at the door to the Jotuns staring at them outside. "My people, the Transformed, will finally be the rulers of this world and solve the problem of mortality that has plagued mankind since time immemorial. The HumanX Project is doomed to fail and the only solution is to give up our humanity and embrace intelligence."

There was a flicker of emotion in his eyes as he spoke fiercely, with eyes, fiery and intense, like those of a fanatic warrior with a cause. Jay suddenly felt certain that Oran was referring to a bigger plan. This man was not playing just a game of war for personal glory, but for something bigger. He was asking for an ideological revolution.

In that next moment, Oran's lips warped into a twisted smile, as he wrapped his hands around Jay's neck like a snake. "Tell me honestly, Jay. Do you want the human race to survive? If you do, don't you agree that embracing intelligence is the only way forward?"

Jay didn't say anything. She felt dull, as the bot's eyes locked onto Jay's. Meanwhile, the delirium led to numbness and Jay felt like she was going to pass out. Was she even breathing? The world around her was so slow, her numbness increasing and yet, her mind actively thinking what to do. But it could not come up with any plan to save her. Instead, all she could think of was the past, and the series of mistakes she made and at that moment, the only person she could think of was her friend, Erol, whom she missed dearly.

And for some strange ironic reason, she saw Erol's face looming outside the window, a hazy shadow visible next to the two Jotuns outside the room. She was probably dreaming, because he was being taken in as a prisoner and yet, his lips were curled up in a smile.

And then, her eyes lit up with hope.

CHAPTER 24

The Rescue

Within a minute, Erol's voice boomed across the room, "Hands up!"

Oran looked back at him with a perplexed expression, as his mouth slowly curved into a vicious smile. Erol snarled back, then charged at him while firing his lasgun. The few shots caught the bot by surprise causing his smile to falter a little, but only managed to graze his chest, ripping off some fabric to reveal a structure of bone, covered by a synthetic bronze-coloured epidermis. Erol stared at him, watching his face register surprise, confusion and then anger in sequence as he drew a much larger lasgun from his own pockets. The bot took aim at Erol who ducked instinctively behind one of the chairs.

"You think your tiny gun can destroy me?" Oran taunted him, then started laughing hysterically. But before Erol could respond to him, Faruk came up from behind, a smirk on his face as he brandished a large Supersonic rifle.

"Not that gun," he said, cocking the rifle. "THIS one."

Oran's laughter ended, his eyes widening as he made for the door. But it was too late. A fraction of a second later, there was a deafening blast from the Supersonic, followed by a crash which toppled Jay and Boro from their chairs.

The world around them had gone black, smoke shrouding the room. The ring of the emergency alarm filled their ears. Erol, who was on his knees, cautiously looked out from behind the chair. There was no movement. A small metal limb covered with a melting prosthetic was visible, sparks flying off it. But it wasn't attached to anything. Oran must have dragged himself out, he thought. Without any more time wasted, Erol crawled over to Jay and began untying her. She was still delirious from the medicine and the explosion, her breathing shallow.

"Jay, wake up. Are you alright?" he asked her.

Still half-dazed, she turned to him, then threw her arms around him. "I am, thanks to you Erol." Tears swelled in her eyes as she hugged him tightly. "I can't believe you're here. How I missed you, Erol!"

"You can thank me later." Erol gently took her hands and helped her get up on her feet. "For now, we have to get going." He looked out the door and saw a few armoured bot guards making their way towards them. Time was running out. He knew he had to do something.

He signalled Faruk. "Faruk, turn on Boro and come help Jay up. I'll deal with those bots."

Faruk nodded as he crawled over to Boro, whose metal body had been lightly charred by the explosion. He quickly reached out to switch on the bot, then proceeded to take out a raspberry pie-shaped device, his hackpad, out and began to access the facility's security systems.

Meanwhile, Erol was trying to plan his offence. There were two Jotuns, both wielding guns charging into the room. As soon as they were in sight, Erol counted till three and lunged forwards, driving a large steel table onto their torsos, the only part that seemed unarmoured. The guards were unable to register the move as the violent impact crushed their pelvic metal cortices, instantly buckling them. With their pelvises cracking from the jarring blow, the Jotuns fell clumsily to the floor, their guns rolling underneath.

"Quick," Erol yelled. "The guns!"

Faruk ran towards the Jotuns, picking their guns up, then stunning them both through a hit on the napes and rewiring them at the calf seams. Finally, he managed to grab one of their IDs.

Not bad, Erol thought, as he wheeled around to check on his friends. Jay was now quite awake, as was Boro, online and alert. But both were still shocked, watching in amazement at the swift rescue operation, and Faruk's ability to disengage the Jotuns.

"This is our cue to leave. We gotto hurry before more show up," Erol said as he helped Jay up.

Meanwhile, Faruk had found a back door in the room. "This way." But the back door appeared to be locked from the outside. The boys kicked at it, but nothing happened. Looking around the large room, Erol noticed a large rod lying on one corner. He grabbed it from the corner and jammed it into the glass window. Nothing happened again. The window was intact, not even a single crack. Meanwhile, Boro walked over to the door and with very little force, he turned on the knob, managing to open it.

Erol stared at him wide-eyed. "How'd you do that? It was locked. *Really* locked!"

"I used my magnetic sensors to unlock it." Then, Boro gave a wry smile.

All of them quickly went out through the back door and were greeted by the stunned faces of human workers and bots. But none of them were wearing uniforms or armour, or even carrying a weapon. They were simply ordinary scientists whose focus was elsewhere.

All of them were walking in the same direction like roaches following food. All except one bot.

Mazu.

He was standing right ahead of them at the end of a corridor, his eyes fixed on all of them.

"Do you know that guy?" Erol asked Jay, worried.

Jay nodded, "I do..." But there was a hint of confusion in her eyes. "I don't know if we can trust him."

"Well then." Erol said, as he pushed them to another corner. "Go, go, go!"

But Mazu was heading towards them. "Wait, Jay." He said with restraint concern. "Let me help you."

Jay stopped but before she could turn, the bot was right behind her.

"I know you're scared, but you must trust me. Once again, you are not safe here. So let me help you all get out of here, back to your family."

Erol grabbed Jay's hand. "We don't even know who you are or why you're here? Why should we trust you?"

Mazu looked at Jay, then at Erol. "There is no other way you all will be safe. I know everything about this place, the layout and security systems. I know the best way to escape, but I need you all to trust me to make it happen."

Jay hesitated. "But you left me and Boro at Raul and Delara's place. We ended up in more danger."

Mazu looked around the Compound anxiously. "We really don't have time. All I can tell you Jay is that I was friends with your parents and I had to do everything to avoid suspicion. I can get you to Salim, your god father."

Jay's eyes lit up when she heard her godfather's name. "Okay, what do we need to do to get to him?"

Mazu sighed, visibly relieved. "First, you have to do exactly as I say. Follow me and keep your heads down. Avoid eye contact with anyone you come across." Mazu said as he looked around the room.

Erol turned to Jay, nudging her. "What is going on? You trust this bot?"

"Not a bot, a cyborg. And he was the first one when we got here. He did help us out." Jay whispered back. Then, she turned suspiciously to Faruk, "And who is that person? In fact, what are you all doing here?"

Erol grinned. "That's Faruk. Faruk waved at her. "He and Dr. Salim came here with me to find you."

Jay frowned. "Salim? As in my uncle? He's *here?*"

Before Erol could reply, Mazu turned around, "Shh. Yes, he's here. Now, heads down. Avoid any eye contact."

Erol turned to Jay. "Let's get to some safe place and I'll tell you all about it."

The kids followed Mazu through the corridors, passing by a number of scientists and bots, but no armoured Jotuns. Besides one or two odd stares, they managed to avoid any contact. They walked all the way into another high-glass tunnel that connected to another building. The building was dark, dilapidated, and cold, with next to no inhabitants.

"What is this place?" Erol asked.

"It's an older building." Mazu said, then looked around and pointed at a door with a stairway sign. "That's it. The fire exit. That will take us to the garage!"

The group followed Mazu out the exit, making their way down to the lowest level they could get to. Three floors below, they came across a reception area with two glass doors leading to a garage-looking space.

One burly man sat at the desk, but he appeared to be asleep. He didn't notice them entering, with his head hunched low and eyes closed.

Using hand gestures, Mazu guided the three kids and Boro to the far end of the garage. Each of them tiptoed past the man in the booth as silently as they could. Mazu was expecting that any second, he would wake up and call out to them, but no such thing happened. He turned around and saw that the man was in the same position as before with no one behind them. He breathed a sigh of relief.

"Is that the only security?" Erol asked. "If so, this place is a joke."

"That's not security." Mazu explained. "That human is there just to greet visitors." Then the bot pointed at the boom gates. *"That* is security."

"What do you mean?" Faruk asked.

"Those are beam-boom gates, that can detect anyone entering or leaving within ten meters, and if they are unable to identify the person, they will alarm the entire Compound."

Jay's face went pale. "How are we going to get out?"

"Leave that to me." Mazu said, but his head seemed to be elsewhere. He was scanning the entire garage and finally took out a handheld device from his pocket.

After some clicks, Mazu was on the call with Azlan.

"The kids are with me in the garage level P2 of the Orka building. No inhabitant in sight"

Then, after a few nods and yesses, Mazu hung up.

"So, what's the plan?" Erol asked.

"The plan is that your guardians have been informed to greet you at the shack where I will be taking you."

"But the gates??" Faruk asked.

"And the Jotuns." Boro added.

"It's all been taken care of." Mazu said, and turned around as a short beep from a small pod within the garage alerted them.

"That's our ride. Now get in it!"

All three kids, Boro and Mazu crammed inside the pod, which self-drove its way to one of the beam-boom gates. They waited in front of the gates, which finally beeped open.

"How did it –" Jay looked at the gate.

"I am operating the consoles – and this pod." Mazu explained. He appeared to be very calm, even though Jay could tell that he had probably never done this before.

"Who are you?" Erol asked, still confused.

Mazu winked at Jay, cuing her to explain.

"Mazu's on our side. He's a cyborg, and when I got here, he was trying to keep me safe from that other bot, Oran." She paused. "There are people called the Syndicate who are running this place and they are conducting some illegal activities. "Jay took a deep breath. "They might be behind my parents' deaths."

Erol did not look as surprised as Jay expected him to be. He sighed. "Salim told me your parents were involved in this place on the way here. He also suspected that your parents may not have died in an accident."

"So, he knew who killed my parents?" Jay sounded hurt.

"No. Not really." Erol said. "He said he just had suspicions that someone murdered them and made it seem like an accident. It was all a suspicion though."

The group became silent after this. Meanwhile, the pod quickly passed through two levels of beam-boom gates until it was out of the parking lot and into the Compound. From there, they took to the further end of the Compound, driving towards the tunnel that went through the border and led to the Res Complex. Jay and Boro remembered it quite well.

Mazu remained calm and cool as they drove towards the border gate. The overhead beam of light from the tower scanned their vehicle. Immediately, the red signal up front turned green, allowing them to proceed forward. Before they knew it, they were already inside the dark tunnel lit up by holograms and neon lights that ran along the length of the tunnel. Inside, it was deathly silent and dark, the lights only allowing them to see a few meters ahead and behind. Soon enough, a faint light marked the end of the tunnel. Minutes later, the pod emerged from the tunnel at an elevated deck looking over the valley that housed the Res Complex. Further to the left was the forest, and much further all around were the hills or the rock barriers that were home to the Makran tunnels.

"You can get up." Mazu announced.

"Why is no one following us?" Jay asked as she saw them get off the highway. "This was unusually smooth for a rescue."

Boro turned to her, after peering outside at the skylight. "Indeed. It appears that someone has made us invisible and disabled the security surveillance system."

All eyes turned to Mazu.

"There is indeed a benefit to being in charge," said the cyborg slyly. "Well, at least until Oran figures out what I have done."

From there, the pod turned right, circling the edge of the valley as it drove in the direction of the forest. They entered the forest from a clear opening, one that only a few people knew off. From there though, the passage was not as straightforward. With a lot of manoeuvring and zig zag actions, the pod made its way through the winding road.

Jay turned to Mazu, "Are you sure no one is following us?"

"No one knows this path." Mazu explained. "Meanwhile, I have sent most of the Jotuns on a goose chase."

"What did you tell them?" Erol asked.

"I've informed the Jotuns that you are posing as scientists and are still in the Compound. Fortunately, with some older footage of Jay, I was able to convince them, but it won't be long until Oran finds out. After that...." Mazu looked at them with a grave expression. "We are all in big trouble."

Jay pursed her lips. "If Oran finds out, what will he do to you?"

"Don't worry about me," Mazu patted her head. "I have evaded certain death quite a few times."

Jay rolled her lips. "Where are you taking us now?"

"The shack." Erol gave her a smug look. "We stayed there with Dr. Salim."

"Will Uncle Salim be there?"

Mazu nodded. "He and Azlan are waiting for you all there. I've informed them. You won't have much time though. You all are to leave as soon as possible. Now, any more questions?"

Boro shrugged and even Jay stopped her tirade of questions. Meanwhile, Mazu drove for another fifteen minutes in a zig zag manner, winding through the trees. As they kept going, Jay noticed that the forest around her had grown increasingly dark with the only source of light to be the pod itself. She looked out the window and saw that the trees were blotting out the sky.

Boro tapped her. "There is no virtual sky here, Jay."

Jay squinted up and noticed no skylight. Boro was correct. She turned to Mazu.

"This is why it's called the Dark Ghaba," Mazu said. "We're almost at the shack."

The trees grew dense as they slowly navigated through the Dark Ghaba. Finally, they saw a small, paved path, which disappeared into a thicket of trees.

"You all get off here." Mazu said as the pod parked itself behind a bushel. "I have to return to make sure that the Jotuns don't find you. Do not leave the shack until I tell you to do so."

All of them disembarked and made their way on to the paved path. There wasn't much they could see, but soon enough, they spotted something up ahead. Nestled among the trees was a dingy ramshackle shack lit up by plasma lamps. They all rushed to it in relief.

CHAPTER 25

The Shack

Salim and Azlan had been anxiously waiting in the shack. As soon as they both heard that Jay had been captured by Oran, that Erol and Faruk had managed to get into the Compound, Salim had possibly lost most of his hair in that short period of time due to worry. His balding spot was now covered in sweat.

"Mazu told me they're all safe," Azlan reminded him. "Don' worry."

Salim looked at him coldly as if he was about to explode.

"Do you even know what it is like, to be responsible for another human being?" screamed Salim. "How could you!? You live alone here!"

"Calm down, Salim. Jeez." Azlan looked at him. "I was jus' trying to comfort you."

"I'm sorry," Salim muttered, "but it's all my fault Jay is here in the first place. I should have known better."

"Don't beat yourself up. She's a smart kid." Azlan got up from the chair he was sitting in and began looking around the shack. On one side of the shack were a series of books. Some of these were purely fun reads that had been smuggled from the overground.

"The shack brings back so many memories." Azlan said.

"Hmmm…," Salim said, feeling a little nostalgic himself, as he let out a deep sigh. "True."

"Reminds me of Jumander, and all our own adventures when we were young...."

Meanwhile, Salim was lost as he stared out into the darkness of the forest. He wondered why they even bothered to have windows in the shack when they could hardly see anything in the Dark Ghaba. But the plasma light from the shack lit up the leaves outside slightly so he could see some of the unique flora outside.

Salim's attention was immediately diverted as he heard some sounds outside. He ran towards the door.

"Dr. Salim!" Erol shouted from outside, "We're here."

Salim's eyes lit up immediately as he opened the door. Erol ran towards the shack, embracing him. Salim looked past him outside and spotted Faruk first, followed by Jay. A wave of intense relief fell over him as soon as he saw his god daughter, his body deflating like a balloon.

"You're all safe," Salim wiped his forehead. "Jay, my sweet girl! Where have you been!?" He waddled up to her and embraced her in a big hug.

Jay didn't say much. She was still more reserved since the last time they had met. But before Salim would enquire the reason for her reservedness, another excited voice erupted from behind him.

Azlan brushed past Salim and took Jay in an embrace.

"There ya' are!" Azlan said as Jay's face was squished to his chest. "Where did you run ov' to, when I gave ya' both clear instructions to stay put?" Azlan glared at Boro.

"Leave her be!" Salim said, then grabbed Jay. "Are you alright?"

"Yes, yes, I am alright," Jay said feeling smothered, "stop squeezing me, both of you!"

"You are never leaving my sight ever again, young lady," Salim finally said.

Jay didn't respond. She looked at him coldly.

"What's the matter, Jay?" Salim asked her.

Jay sighed. "Why didn't you tell me about all this?"

Salim's face turned pale. He turned to Azlan, who nodded and only offered two words. "She knows."

Salim closed his eyes unsure of what to say. He had already pushed Jay away once. He couldn't do it again.

"Jay, I'm sorry..." Salim managed to say. "I had made a promise to your parents that I'd keep you safe. After their disappearance, I felt that the best way to keep you safe was to keep you unaware of Gedrosia."

"So you lied about who my parents were?" Jay said, more sad than angry.

No sooner had Jay said this, she realized everyone had their heads turned towards them. Salim coughed uncomfortably as others in the room moved to a corner to afford them some privacy.

"I...yes, I did." Salim did not want to make any excuses. "I didn't tell you about who they really were. They were archaeologists, but just involved in some very top-secret projects."

Tears oozed down Jay's eyes. "But you should have told me something! For the longest time, I thought they left me purposely, that they deserted me."

"Come here, child," Salim said as he pulled Jahan towards him. "I'm sorry for hiding this."

Briefly, the two embraced when Salim remembered the box that Mazu had provided him.

"Wait here," Salim whispered to Jay as he kissed her forehead. He left to look inside the shack and retrieve the cardboard box for her.

"Jay," Salim looked up at Jay, "Mazu gave this to me today. It's a box containing your mother and father's belongings. I shouldn't be telling you this, but I am not going to keep this from you any longer. Your parents were involved in setting up Gedrosia and when your father wanted to shut down the Syndicate, he disappeared. It wasn't an accident. It was the Syndicate who were behind their death." Salim's eyes were slowly brimming with tears again. "I never knew the full truth either. I imagine this is what you must have felt too a few months ago, when you found that journal. You see, I've been duped to. Your parents were doing more here in Gedrosia than I imagined. But they wanted to fix it and they were murdered for that."

Jay buried her head in Salim's as she sobbed.

"I'm sorry, my child," Salim kissed Jay on her head. Then, he took out an envelope from the box. "This is a message they left for you. It seems they knew the risks of what they were doing."

Jay started weeping as soon as she took the letter, and held on tight to Salim, as both girl and guardian bawled their eyes out.

***

Tears were followed by sounds of laughter in a tiny shack in a forgotten part of Gedrosia. For a mere second, the world had ceased to exist for the residents of that shack who recollected parts of their connected past.

"What were they like?" Jay asked them, "my parents, I mean."

"Your parents?" Azlan sighed settling back in the seat looking in empty space as if reflecting at the memory. "Both of 'em were involved in Gedrosia early on. Your mum was a renowned scientist, always buried in some obtuse research. Do you know that she's the one who led the recruitment efforts in Gedrosia?"

"No," Jay said, "I had no idea."

"Your father, Jumander, very charismatic… and bossy," Azlan said.

"Now I know who Jay takes after." Erol joked.

Everyone laughed.

"Why was my father worried about the Syndicate?" Jay asked. Her eyes shifted between Azlan and Salim who were hesitant to say much.

Azlan sighed. "Your parents, brilliant people, Jay." As he said this, there was a sad, sympathetic edge to his voice. "They started off like most ov' us, thinking this'd be a noble mission. When you were born, they decided to leave Gedrosia and move to Kolachi to raise you, away from all this. It was also 'round that time something happened between the Syndicate and your father. He confronted them and wanted to expose them, but the Syndicate took action against them first."

"What did they find out?" Faruk asked.

Mazu explained, "There were things happening in the Syndicate, enhancements among other things, that they found unethical. That's the extent of information we have."

"That's it? That's all you know? Jay muttered. "Or is there more?" She remembered these events so vividly as if they had just happened. She was five years old, playing in her house with Hikmah when Uncle Salim had come to her, informing her that her parents would be gone for a few days. Days had turned into months, and months into years until Uncle Salim finally told her that they would not be coming back. They were gone.

"It is quite likely that your parents may have felt guilty working with the Syndicate and knew about the Syndicate's plans all along," Azlan said bluntly.

Salim then added, "Even if they were involved in some form or manner, the Jumander's I knew stood up for progress, not for secrecy and war. They may have known about the possibility of enhancements, but they'd have only worked on it to advance humankind's progress. They would never however, harm another soul."

Jay felt empty, broken as she tried to recreate the image of her parents. For long, she had imagined them to be ordinary archaeologists that encountered misfortune while conducting an excavation. But the truth was far from that. They were covert operators, working in a top-secret underground facility that was conducting questionable research. Still, they may not have been all good, but they didn't deserve to die.

"So the Syndicate killed them over enhancements?" Jay asked. Her bluntness about her parents surprised Salim.

"Well, they might've been doing something more horrendous than just enhancements." Azlan said. "Perhaps, very advanced cyborgs?"

"Cyborgs?" Erol erupted. "You mean like Oran and Mazu?"

"You could tell they are cyborgs?" Salim turned to the boy, then Jay and Faruk. All three shook their heads, one by one.

"It was obvious that they were more than bots. Their movements, expressions... *texture*. We grew up around bots so we notice these distinctions." Erol said. "Anyways, what is so wrong about them? Cyborgs?"

Salim hesitated to say more but he knew the questions would just keep coming. "Kids, there is some dangerous process that is going on, experimentation on humans without their consent. The idea is to make humans into cyborgs that can reproduce and eventually replace the original human race."

Jay had her eureka moment there. "So that is what Oran was talking about! He spoke about replacing the human race, to make a new race of advanced beings. The syndicate wanted the Transformed to be the rulers of this world. He said that the only way to solve the problem of mortality was to embrace intelligence."

"Too bad we have no proof of what the Syndicate it up to," said Azlan. "At least not enough."

"Wait a minute," Jay exclaimed as she turned to Boro. "Do you have that chip? The one that …that thing… in the tunnels gave us?"

Boro walked up to them and placed the chip on the table.

"What is it?" Azlan asked.

"We are not sure of the contents of this chip," Boro said.

Jay added, "When we left your home, we ended up falling into one of the tunnels that collapsed. I can't really recall how we got there, but it wasn't far from there. We saw a creature that said that this is where the transformed failed."

Before they could discuss this further, the door of the shack opened in complete surprise. Shock was followed by relief as they saw Mazu enter.

"Time to go everyone. There is a search underway all over Gedrosia - for Jay and her friends. Which means we all need to get out of here. Now."

"Now, now?" Salim said.

"Yes." Mazu said, "which means Azlan needs to very quickly find us a route through the tunnels."

Jay raised her eyebrows, then quickly took out the books she'd taken from Azlan's home from her bag. "These might be of help then."

"I was wondering why my bookshelf seemed off," Azlan snatched the books from Jay's hand. "Little rascal you!"

Jay smiled sheepishly. "Boro and I have studied the exits. I think most of these are blocked though."

"We are taking an exit through the tunnels. No one knows about it."

"The CAECA-2 exit?" Boro asked "I believe there is uncertainty around its existence. I have found that it has been mentioned in only one map, while erased from the rest of the maps. I have studied them all in great detail."

"Certainly exists!" Azlan added. "I designed it."

"Can we debate this later?" Mazu said firmly. "We have no time for chit chat."

Azlan got up from the table. "Orit. What is the plan?"

Mazu gave a firm nod. "Azlan, you take Salim and the kids to the exit, CAECA-2, or whichever exit is not blocked." Then, Mazu turned to Salim, "Salim, there will be a copter waiting for you overground by 7:00 am tomorrow. That gives you all around six hours to escape."

"And what about you?" Azlan asked Mazu.

Mazu looked at his wristpad. "I don't have much time, but I have to get back to the forest and plan a diversion for you all." He momentarily paused. "I might even need to figure out an evacuation plan for the other scientists here." He looked up at all of them. "Is that clear?"

Azlan looked at him for a bit, then shook his head.

"Whose Compactor is out front?"

"That's mine." Salim said.

"Great. Use that to get to the tunnels. I'll follow behind..." Mazu slapped both his hands, "Let's move," he said impatiently. "We're not going to accomplish anything by standing around here talking about it."

Salim, Azlan and the kids all sighed in unison, as they went along with the proposed plan, unsure how exactly it would pan out. There were still many questions left unanswered, but they all knew now was not the time. Right now, the only thing they all needed to focus on was the escape. Even with all the intricacies involved in their plan, they knew that the best way forward was to simply go ahead with those who knew Gedrosia best.

210

CHAPTER 26

Final Escape

The Landstorm made its way through the thicket of trees, entering the wild Gedrosian jungle. Another smaller pod followed behind, the Compactor, with a balding professor and three raggedy kids as its excited passengers. After half an hour of very difficult maneuvering through the trees, both the pods arrived at what appeared to be the edge of the Dark Ghaba. Up ahead, the trees were beginning to thin out and the rock ceiling had been replaced by the hologram-lit azure sky, bright and visible through the branches. A mile or so further, a clearing was visible that led up to a cliff drop.

The first pod halted before the clearing, burrowing behind a bushel of trees; the other pod also settled behind the first. Azlan and Boro emerged from the first pod, leaving the cover of the forest and slowly made their way into the clearing, stopping before a sheer thirty feet drop to the ground. They scanned the area for Jotuns, and then inspected their vantage point. To their right, the clearing ascended further, ending in a much steeper bluff; to the left, it went down like a ramp for miles and miles, rolling around the hill and then, disappearing behind more trees.

Azlan made his way to the professor in the other pod.

"All clear?" Salim rolled his windows down.

Azlan nodded. "Come out with me but leave the kids inside." After some complaining grunts from the passengers, he added a qualifier, "For now."

Salim shook his head in acquiescence. As he got out, he looked around the forest. "Is this where CAECA-2 is?"

"No, but it's close."

"Oh, I see…" Salim hesitated.

Azlan smirked, sensing his apprehension. "Don't worry. I know where it is. Follow me."

"Whatever you say," Salim muttered under his breath.

Both of them skirted back to the edge of the clearing where Boro awaited them at the cliff drop.

"There!" Azlan said, as he pointed at the opposite side of the cliff where another conjoined hill rose from the ground. "That's where CAECA-2 is." Then, he pointed to the left. "This side of the bluff descends to ground level and can get us across."

"That," Boro said with some concern, as he edged towards the cliff, fixated on what was below the cliff. "And an army of Jotuns."

"What did you say, Boro?" Salim almost shirked, but avoided to say anything further. He crawled his way to the edge drop and peeped out. It didn't take long for him to see what was happening.

A congregation of Jotuns had just rounded the hill. Rows and rows of perhaps hundred fully armoured Jotuns were marching along, then proceeding to stop at the edge of the hill.

"What do we do now?" Salim turned to Azlan in worry.

Azlan exchanged glances with Boro, then took a deep breath. "Our best bet's to speak to Mazu right now."

"But Mazu would be busy. He was supposed to distract Oran and his Jotuns."

"Yes, but we've no choice. This could well be a trap to lure us out. In either case, we can't go to the tunnel right now."

✳ ✳ ✳

Back in the pod, Jay was growing restless as she watched Azlan, Salim and Boro out in the clearing formulating some plan. Meanwhile, the forest around them had grown deathly silent. Even the steady drone of unusual insects had ceased.

"What do you think they're planning?" Jay asked, peeping out the window.

"Beats me but whatever it is, I hope they decide soon," Erol rubbed his stomach. "I'm hungry."

"That makes the two of us," said Faruk as his stomach let out a loud groan. "I didn't know we would need to ration food here."

Jay looked at hungry Erol and Faruk, then back at the clearing. Aha! She just found herself an opportunity to leave the pod! "Well, perhaps I'll go and ask them how much longer it is. After all, you guys look pretty hungry."

"But Dr. Salim told us to wait in the pod," Erol said apprehensively.

"Yeah, I can wait." Faruk added.

Jay seemed anxious. "I feel like we've waited long enough."

Before Erol or Faruk could stop her, Jay got out of the pod making her way to the clearing behind the ledge. Erol and Faruk hastily followed.

Just as all three of them walked out into the forest, a strange buzzing sound engulfed them all. The sound continued to grow louder and louder. Frozen, all three looked up at what was making the sounds. Their breaths held, they saw gigantic butterflies fluttering over them, their curious eyes centred on each of the boys as they drew closer. They were mammoth, their wings spanning the length of a human.

"You all need to get back in the pod," Salim shouted from afar.

Azlan turned to the kids, shouting, "Whatever ya' do, don't move!"

But it was too late. Faruk had gotten hold of his lasgun and was pointing it towards the butterflies. With his eyes closed, he was ready to shoot but before he could, Azlan had grabbed the gun and flashed an orblight in front of the butterflies. Then, he threw the light further away. The butterflies immediately flew towards it far into the depths of the forest.

"They're only insects," said Azlan. "They won't harm you and if you intimidate them, we would have more insects attack. Now come on, all three ov' you!"

The group continued through the clearing, and as the giant butterflies flew away, the kids ran towards Salim and Boro, at the ledge.

"I told you to stay inside the pod," Salim sounded upset.

"We were hungry," Erol replied as he covered for Jay.

Salim sighed. "Well, now that you are here, I might as well let you know that we might need to wait until the Jotuns clear the entrance to CAECA-2."

The kids looked confused, but then leaned towards the ledge and looked down at the congregation of Jotuns.

There were quiet gasps.

"What will we do now?" Jay asked.

Salim turned to Azlan, who seemed to be busy on his paging device.

Then, they all turned their attention elsewhere.

***

There was some ruffling in the leaves from the forest behind them.

Azlan stood still, then crouched below a bush as he signalled the others to stay back. All the others hid behind a large boulder on the ledge.

The ruffling continued, closer and closer until a silhouette was visible behind a tree. There was pin drop silence.

Then there was a sigh.

It was Mazu.

Quickly, Azlan got up from his crouched position and ran up to him, with Salim, Boro and the three kids joining behind.

"I'm so glad it's you!" Azlan said without a break. "We're in a pickle, you won't believe what I'm about to tell you." Azlan stopped talking as he noticed something was off.

Mazu looked quiet and grim.

"What's wrong, Mazu?" Azlan asked.

Before Mazu could answer, another shuffling of leaves followed. This time, there was gasps.

Oran came out of the forest.

✳✳✳

No one said a word for a brief moment of time. There was shock, despair and hopelessness but no one said anything.

"What do you want?" Azlan finally said.

"What do *I* want?" Oran let out a laugh. "I want all of you dead."

Salim and Boro shielded all the three kids who scurried behind the professor and the bot.

"Let these kids go," Azlan said.

"They have done nothing wrong," Mazu said as he turned towards Oran.

"You, traitor, stop speaking," Oran looked furious.

"Then, let them go for your family's sake." Azlan said.

Oran's eyes reddened as he raised his lasgun towards Azlan. "Do not ever mention my family! Else, I will kill everyone near or dear to you."

Salim walked up to Oran, as Jay tried to hold him back.

"Listen, Idris. We are not the enemies." Salim said. "You know the people responsible for your misery. The people who took your family are the same people who took Jay's."

"Jay's father started it all." Oran finally said. "He's the one who started this sanctuary, and he's the one responsible for a lot of the problems."

Azlan and Salim were quiet. Jay had tears in her eyes, but she wiped them and came forward to stand beside Salim.

"You're right. He took away a lot from you. He also took away a lot from me. My own father did not tell me anything about Gedrosia. But that's why I must fix what he did wrong. I must end what he started. Please, Oran, no Idris. Give me that chance. You and I are alike. We both have been wronged."

Oran/Idris's eyes were flickering, as if there was some thought process happening behind them.

Mazu put his hands around Oran's shoulder. "We know who you are, Idris, and it's not this. You are a compassionate man, who loved his family and whose life was taken away from the overground. We are beside you, and will see to it that the perpetrators who took your family from you, are brought to justice."

Idris/Oran turned to Mazu. "How do you plan to do that?"

Mazu turned to Salim, who cleared his throat and started speaking. "I know Moira Harper very well. I will plan to take this information about the Syndicate to her. If you, Idris, can help us in this mission, I guarantee you that not only will you be provided protection and amnesty, but that there will be an investigation into the mobsters behind your wife and daughter's murder." Salim paused. "I give you my word, Idris."

"You deserve justice." Azlan added, "Your family deserves justice. Let us help with that."

Idris seemed to be more human this time, almost as if the cyborg in him had shut down. He lowered his lasgun.

"It's too late." He sighed, "The Jotuns are already on their way, and they have directions from the Syndicate. Even if I helped you escape now, it's only a matter of time that the Syndicate would find you."

"Not before we bring it down," Jay stepped forward. She put her hand in her pocket and took out a small chip. "I have incriminating evidence. Once the UR sees this, the Syndicate will be shut down."

Idris frowned. Jay and the others held their breaths, unsure at what the human/cyborg would do next.

"Go, then." Idris finally said. "On my signal, you all must run. I will try to distract the Jotuns meanwhile."

"What signal?" Azlan said, relieved.

"You will know. Now, no more questions. Just be ready. Idris was about to leave but Mazu embraced him. "Thank you. For everything."

Idris nodded as he turned down the descending clearing to make his way to the Jotuns.

※※※

All of them were huddled behind the ledge as they waited for the signal. They had no idea what that signal was but they figured, they'd know it when they saw it. Or at least one of the six would.

They watched Idris reach the congregation of Jotuns, who were all guarding the barrier wall. Idris was ordering something to them, but neither of them were budging. Another human scientist, who nobody could recognize, walked up to Idris. They both were arguing, and then they saw Idris raise his lasgun on the human's head. Then, there was a shot.

The kids gasped. Salim told them all to turn away. The congregation of bots were walking away. Azlan turned to them all. "That's our signal!"

The first thing they had to do was to get to the barrier wall. The wall ran parallel to the elevated ledge they were on. It was easy to get to from one corner of the ledge, which went down like a ramp, connecting them to the basin below. Azlan and Mazu were the first to walk to the side of the ledge, which sloped downwards, to reach the same level as where the congregation was.

"Is that man dead?" Faruk asked Dr Salim, as they followed Azlan and Mazu.

Salim shook his head. "No, he was only shot in the leg. He'll live."

"Who was he?" Erol asked, gulping.

"No one to concern yourself with," said Mazu. "Now, let's move quickly."

At the ground level, the congregation was turned away from them, heading in another direction. Fortunately, no one sparked any attention at all and luckily for them, there was a slight curve in the hill that allowed them to hide at a certain angle.

As soon as they reached the wall barrier, Azlan and Mazu began inspecting it. Azlan's movement was sporadic and quick, left to right and then stabilized until he found a hollow spot in the wall.

"This is it, Mazu."

Mazu nodded at Azlan, who gave the wall a firm rap with his metal knuckles, and the sound came back in an echo.

"The cave entrance!" Jay said.

Azlan and Mazu exchanged glances, then the cyborg struck at it hard. The moment he slashed the wall, it cracked and broke away almost like cardboard as several pieces of loose stone came out in his hands.

All of them jumped at the sound, which echoed in the small valley. Jay and the kids looked around, then saw the congregation that seemed to have moved quite further away. They were relieved.

But only momentarily.

One Jotun had stopped in his tracks and was slowly turning around. He had heard them.

"Quickly, go in. Now!" Azlan yelled as he saw the Jotun turn.

"But the Jotun saw us!" Jay yelled.

"Doesn't matter. We keep going." Azlan grabbed the children and pushed them through the tunnel. Salim followed behind.

Mazu took out his lasgun and turned around to face the Jotuns. "I'll stay back to guard."

Azlan nodded. "Okay. Stay in touch."

Then, along with Boro, he crawled into the hole last, hearing more shots.

Faraway shots.

CHAPTER 27

CAECA -2

The passage had a strange chill, reminding them of a power that was ancient but untouched. The opening, it appeared had been carved, rather than naturally formed. Unlike some of the other Makran tunnels, this one lacked the smoothness of the walls. The walls were rugged. And there was no gypsum lining the walls. The only light was from the outside, which fell into the cave for about ten feet.

Then, there was only darkness.

The children were on all fours, rushing inside, paying no heed to the darkness. Salim was following behind, making sure they kept going.

The passage had narrowed into a circular, smooth tunnel, causing them all to crouch more tightly.

Slowly, as they all creeped in, the strange silence and darkness intensified their fear. Though the changes were subtle, they could all sense that the tight walls were beginning to close in around them. The air grew thicker and harder to breathe, and a feeling of claustrophobia began to settle over the group.

"Dr. Salim?" Erol turned back to the professor, brows sweating.

"Yes, Erol?"

"This tunnel is ... very dark. Are you sure it will lead us out?"

Salim looked at the other kids and could see their faces growing pale with sheer fear and panic. They were beginning to feel trapped in the ever-tightening confines of the tunnel.

Salim turned around to Azlan, who looked at all of them calmly. "It *will* open up. We just need to get through this tight patch. Take deep breaths."

The group stumbled forward, their hearts pounding and their breaths coming in short gasps.

Azlan turned to Salim and whispered. "You need to get them to calm down. The tunnel is safe but they all need to keep their panic at bay. Otherwise, they could get hurt."

Salim gulped. He was dealing with his own fears: the fear that this mission would fail, the fear that they would not be able to find the exit and even the fear of how to get back home once they made it back to the surface of the desert. The knowledge of this failed escape gnawed at him, as the tunnel gnawed into the earth's bowels. But he took a deep breath. Luckily, he knew how to manage panic attacks.

Salim closed his eyes. "Everyone, do what I say," he said. His voice was calm and soothing, as he radiated a sense of confidence and reassurance, despite his internal fear.

"First of all," he said, "Take slow, deep breaths in through your nose and out through your mouth. Focus on your breathing. Do not think about anything else. If you can't focus on your breathing, think about what you want to do once you get overground. Think about what you want to play, what you want to eat..." The group seemed to be listening attentively and the panting-wheezing sounds seemed to have stopped.

The caravan moved on, despite their trepidations. They proceeded deeper into the tunnel, their breathing calmer than before, even though the air was permeated with a raw, stuffy smell. After an unknown amount of time had passed, the air finally began to carry traces of fresh air. As if urged forth by a hope that there was an opening, all of them increased their pace. And in the short span of about three deep breaths, they arrived at a junction point in the tunnel. To the right, the tunnel continued a few more steps, emptying into a basin chamber while the second path continued as a narrow tunnel, disappearing into the darkness.

"Which way do we go from here?" Jay asked Azlan.

Before he could reply, Erol pushed everyone aside, panting heavily as he ran towards the basin chamber to the right.

The others were quick to follow him into the airier chamber, a large cavern only lit up by some light coming at the end where it continued on further as a narrower tunnel. Although apprehensive, all of them rested in the chamber, and for the first time in a while, had a chance to relax, even if it was even for a second.

"We made it." Erol said. "I don't know about you all, but that was really rough."

"It was just a panic attack," Salim explained. "It happens to everyone. I am proud of you all for getting through this."

Then, Salim turned to Azlan, "Where to, now?"

Azlan looked around the chamber, an initial skepticism quickly replaced with projected confidence.

"This way," he said as he pointed in the direction of a dark passage at the far end of the chamber. They walked up to it and examined it. From the looks of it, it wasn't exactly a tunnel, but a jagged-looking passage with rock outcrops from all corners. However, unlike the earlier tunnel, it was much wider and had a slight draft coming from it.

Salim took a step into it. "I think you're right. I feel some incoming air."

Boro turned to the group. "We need to decide quickly," he said. "It is 8 am already, and we all must make it out before 9 am."

Azlan sighed. "Let's go then. It shouldn't be much longer."

Boro shook his head. "Then, let's proceed."

Faruk, who was examining the smaller tunnel they had come out from, turned to them in worry.

"Hurry guys...I hear some footsteps, something behind us, from the narrow tunnel."

Salim looked at Azlan, worried. "I thought Mazu would take care of the Jotuns."

Azlan took another deep breath. "Y'all keep going through this passage. I'm going to stay here to make sure no one gets through." Azlan turned to Boro, "Boro, you can find the way out, right?"

The bot nodded as he led them all into the passage. Azlan took out a lasgun and slowly backed into the opening of the narrow tunnel, keeping an eye on any movements.

Then, they all heard a shot.

CHAPTER 28

Incoming

It began with a single shot. The sudden, loud echo of a lasgun reverberated off the caves' walls, warning them of the approaching Jotuns. Then, from high above them—and soon enough, from all around them—they heard shots and metal clangs enveloping them as they grew in intensity.

Everyone stared at Azlan blankly until he yelled at them in angry disbelief. "What're y'all waiting for? Go now!! I'll hold 'em off."

Without another word, the entire group ran through the passage, hands stretched out before them in the darkness, with the desperate hope that they would make it out alive.

Meanwhile, Azlan hid behind the rocky outcrops of the chamber, instinctively crouching down low, as he peeked to look back to where the shots were coming from.

He could see the approaching black shadows.

Azlan turned around to the passage to see the kids and they were well out of sight. And hopefully on their way home. He sighed in relief, then still hidden behind the rock, he took out a grenade from his pocket.

He watched them. The two Jotuns had clearly struggled to crawl their way into the chamber. They seemed disoriented and as soon as they circled around with their backs towards Azlan, Azlan came out from hiding, leapt onto the bots and smacked each of them on the spinal switch in their nape, freezing them for a few seconds.

Quickly, Azlan performed a quick surgery to shut down the two bots, who were all frozen in their positions. Once the Jotuns were fully shut down, Azlan looked back into the narrow tunnel to see if others were following. Though there were no signs of other Jotuns approaching, he knew this security would be short-lived.

* * *

As they crept through the passage, Salim felt the sweat coming down his forehead. The sound of mechanical footsteps was audible now, but he wasn't sure where it was coming from.

"Come on, guys, we need to move faster," he whispered urgently to the group in front of him. "They're right on our tail. We all need to pick up the pace."

Salim could hear the others panting and gasping for breath as they stumbled through the darkness, but he was pushing them on. "Come on, just a little bit further."

Jay turned around and gave him an angry glare. "We are all going as fast as we can."

Salim wiped the sweat of his forehead as he kept going. Further ahead, the tunnel levelled and opened into a wider chamber of rocky outcrops. Two other tunnels emerged from this chamber, one with a continuing ascent and another which remained as a flat, dark tunnel. Without much verbal exchange, Boro pointed at the ascending tunnel, and the others nodded in acquiescence.

The group was now on its way into the narrow, ascending tunnel, but the worst was yet to come. Just seconds into the tunnel, they heard another shot. Except this shot came from right behind them.

"Boro, you stay back with me in this chamber and let the kids go."

The bot crawled his way back to Salim's side.

"You all need to keep going. We are going to make sure no one follows."

"But we don't know where to go." Erol protested.

"You have to come with us," Jay was almost teary eyed.

"I promise, I will follow. I just need to stay back to make sure you all aren't pursued."

Jay was crying now.

"Go NOW. Erol take her." Salim shouted.

Erol and Faruk nudged at Jay as the three continued into the ascending tunnel. The incline grew steeper until they were back to crawling, rather climbing the floor. Erol craned out his neck, staring ahead to see if the incline would continue as is, which appeared as if vertical, but he didn't falter in her movements lest it destroy the confidence of the others following him.

Meanwhile, Salim and Boro stayed behind, awaiting any Jotuns. But then, from out of nowhere, they saw Azlan's shadow appear into the chamber. He turned around and stuck his gun out, firing three shots back into the passage he had come out from.

All of them dove for cover.

Then, a deafening explosion ripped through the underground chamber. Azlan was knocked to his knees. Even Salim and Boro, who were crouching near to the end of the chamber were knocked over. But as Azlan struggled back to his feet, another sound caused him to look up. Rock began to fall. He looked around the chamber, and to the end, he caught sight of Salim and Boro.

"What in the hell is happening!?" Salim shouted at him.

"What do you think? The Jotuns are trying to get into this tunnel. And if they can't get through due to their size, they might bring all of it down." Azlan then shouted at Salim, "Why are you still here? You need to leave or all this will be in vain."

Salim didn't answer. "I thought you might need my help. Do you have an extra gun for myself and Boro?"

"I don't know," Azlan said as he stood up. He looked disoriented, and then finally took out another lasgun out of his back pocket. "This will suffice. Not so powerful but aim at the nape and it might stun the bots." Azlan handed one to Salim.

All three had now taken cover behind rocky outcrops they found in the chamber and kept taking turns looking back and forth, for danger. Meanwhile, as they waited at the far end for more Jotuns, Salim asked Azlan with an unusual sense of perceptiveness asked, "Have you thought about death?"

Azlan looked back at him stunned. "Yes! Can we talk about it later? I would rather not think about it now, especially when the chances of it are high."

It didn't look like Salim noticed the stress that Azlan was facing. "Well, I've been thinking... even if we don't die now, we will likely die *without* the sanctuaries. You see, even if we save innocent lives now, they'll still die sooner or later."

Azlan looked peeved. "Well, let's rather have it later, okay? And anyway, I don't fully buy the HumanX findings."

"You don't? Why?" Salim seemed more concerned with his friend's answer than the threat of the wall collapsing on them or the impending danger from the Jotuns.

Azlan bent down, shot into the open space ahead, and then without leaving his aim and sight, he said, "I don't believe a model of interdependency. No matter what numbers may say, oddly life finds a way and I think humans too will find a way." Azlan paused and looked over his shoulder. "All clear. Let's start walking slowly through the ascent."

Salim sighed. "I wish I shared your optimism. But you are a numbers guy. You should understand the low probability of survival. Alas, I'm a scientist."

Peeved, even more, Azlan exclaimed, "If you are a scientist, then you also understand variables. Salim, the ENO2 predictions have no variable for adaptability. Living things and human beings in particular have adapted to many natural phenomena in the past but adaptability was never included in this model. Humans *always* find a way to adapt, don't they? They'll develop alternative food sources or reposition their diets. They'll find the vaccines for diseases. They'll adapt. That's what we do. We may not thrive, but we might survive."

"I suppose." Salim said, his voice somewhat hesitant. He did though feel a little ridiculous that as a scientist, he never challenged or investigated the ENO2 findings, especially as they led to such authoritarian laws, and then, this sanctuary model. He wondered if his pondering at this moment was due to lack of oxygen.

Salim silently reflected, while Azlan was looking all around, shooting in the direction of the passage behind them. Finally, he turned to Boro and Salim, "You both need to go now. Salim, you can meditate once you are safe. This tunnel is going to collapse at any moment."

"What are you saying?" Salim said, awaking from his trance.

Azlan was about to say something when a sudden jolt knocked all three of them to their knees. The tremor also knocked down all the pursuing bots.

Azlan took out a hand grenade. "Get out now!" He pushed Salim and Boro forward into the ascending tunnel and began to shoot at the walls ahead. Salim and Boro hesitated for a while, and with an angry look from Azlan, left to catch up with the others.

***

A few minutes later, there was a deafening explosion. It was the grenade. The shock wave that it created would have brought down the Jotuns. Salim looked back and what he saw next confirmed his fears. The rock formations in the roof of the chamber had begun to break down. Almost frozen, Salim wondered if he could save Azlan but before he could move, Boro grabbed him and dragged him forward.

"Come on, Salim!" Boro shouted above the din of falling stone. "I'd say it's time we got out of here!"

They both continued running and then crawling upwards as fast as they could until they caught sight of the children, who were ahead of them. Their joy of reunion was short-lived as they all noticed the tremors in the ground and the debris falling from the ceiling.

"The tunnel...!" Jay shouted. "It's collapsing!"

"Go. Keep going." Salim ordered and pushed them all.

"But where's Azlan?" Jay asked. Without a reply from Salim, Jay shouted in a panic-stricken voice, "Are we gonna leave him to die?"

"Just keep going or we will all die!"

His statement didn't help because Faruk now yelled, "What? Are we gonna die?"

Salim this time yelled at them. "Keep moving. NOW. That is an order!"

As he had expected, all of them tuned their faces away and continued the steep ascent. Finally, much to their relief, they saw the tunnel levelling up, the light getting brighter. As they all arrived at a levelled tunnel area, they saw it. A hole in the ceiling where sunlight was pouring through and the desert's heat pierced inside.

It didn't take them long to figure out how to climb up. Boro jumped up through the opening, then lowered his hands to get each human out one by one.

They were all alive and outside. At last.

***

As the crew made its exit out of the tunnel, the battle continued in the cave between Azlan and the Jotuns. No one could see anything, the shoot-out taking place in utter darkness. The tremors had heightened, and very soon, Azlan and any of the Syndicate's bots forgot about each other as they all scrambled for cover.

Then, weakened by the shock wave of the explosion, and the collapse of the wall, more rocks began to crack. The main outcrop accompanied by huge slabs of stone rained down onto the chamber floor. With the immense load above no longer evenly supported, all the rocks began to crack and crumble in a domino effect, escalating into a maelstrom of destruction. The falling ceiling however, revealed a hollow space. Whether it was a tunnel, Azlan was not sure, but he ran towards it, knowing this would be his one and only chance.

CHAPTER 29

Leaving Gedrosia

A grey helicopter roared to a landing at the end of an elevated stretch in the desert. As the blades slowed to a visible speed, the rear cargo door opened, and an unusually tall man jumped out. Dressed in a loose shirt and jeans, the man walked coolly up to them, his cheap, shiny shades and shaggy thick hair made him seem like a young lad. He waved at Salim, barely evading the rotor blade as he jogged out to meet them.

"You must be Doctor Salim? Mazu informed me all about you," the young man thrust his hand forward. "Kahn Klaus, at your service." He made a low bow so that his shades almost came off. Salim couldn't help but roll his eyes, while the three teenagers chuckled.

"Hello Kahn. I'm Salim Sarmo. Here with me are Jahan Jumander, Erol Ehmet, and Faruk Ibad." After a pause, he uttered, "And this here is their bot, Boro."

"Glad to meet you all. We must proceed quickly now."

They shook hands, and suddenly the helicopter roared back to life, making them all jump. It was the first time Jay was so close to a helicopter, and she had no idea if she were even going to sit on it.

"Are you the only one they sent?" Salim asked as he looked carefully at Kahn.

Kahn nodded. Then, Salim also looked at the helicopter. "How did you guys afford that thing, anyway?"

Kahn gave a smug grin. "Ah, the chopper, well, there are many people who keep an eye on Gedrosia, the diplomats and others. And some of them are pretty rich so they let us use these things when needed..."

"Well, the rich folks could probably have afforded to send more support staff. Are you the only one they sent for our "rescue"?

Kahn became red. "Well, yes. I'm all there is from the Overground end. But there are others on standby to support evacuation should some evidence present itself."

Salim frowned. "Evidence?" Then he turned to Jay who took out a chip out of her pocket.

"Perhaps you might want to ready those on standby."

"Yes sir," Kahn said, as he stared at the chip, then guided them all to the chopper as they flew away from the underground horrors.

CHAPTER 30

Aftermath

Months had passed and there was still confusion about why there were so many members of the UR in the Makran region. Most analysts assumed it was another peacekeeping effort. But what conflict was it this time?

Experts weighed in. The reason for their presence was an ongoing investigation around radical bots and the RAD virus. Others offered a similar reasoning: A cleanup effort of bot remnants and the Alpha chip was what warranted the UR's presence in the region.

Even other analysts have gone on to make bolder, political statements. They say that the Indus government has misled the people of the Unit. They have deceived them into believing they are safe whereas they are not. There are radical bots capable of robo-terrorism in the wastelands, as well as on the Mashkid Unit and maybe even the Gangetic Unit. These analysts are now calling for closing of borders and saying NO to all refugees – human or bot.

But how does this explain one odd thing: the students and the professor. Apparently, the UR had mysteriously rescued a professor, and three children, likely his students, from the Makran region. The three minors were chaperoned by a bot and had gotten lost in the desert while in search of some archaeological remnants. What is indeed odder is that the UR is providing them a handsome stipend. Is that payment for their secrecy? Journalists believe so. What is the UR hiding?

233

The rescued kids were questioned by media and even some intelligentsia. Time and time again, they were asked if the UR was hiding something. Whether there is some cover up. Perhaps the CHB has something to do with it? Some even mentioned an outrageous story about a sanctuary. They were the same questions being asked over and over again.

Some journalists have interviewed Mrs. Rani, a guesthouse owner in Pasni, who knows two of the kids quite well and is also aware of their expedition. She has claimed that one of the kids is her future daughter-in-law.

Journalists have also managed to interview the parents of one of the kids, Faruk Ibad. Faruk belongs to a family of humble origins, and is a first-generation college student.

"We are very proud of our son." The parents have been reported saying.

"Why are you proud of him?"

"He's on a scholarship and we know he's been involved in a top-secret mission with the UR."

"Do you know anything about it?"

"Well, it's top secret."

Under these secretive circumstances, journalist have only been able to create a piecemeal story about what has happened while conspiracies continue to float. In all this, the UR has chosen to remain silent. It has decided not to interfere in Unit politics. However, due to the growing call for borders, it has conveyed a message: No Unit government can dispose of refugees, humans or bots, or make statements that could be perceived as xenophobic. They simply did not permit it.

Eventually, blame had been deflected onto the CHB Syndicate, most likely from some insider. It was too clandestine an organization with no public accountability. How could it be a part of the UR? Where did it get the funding? Who were the private entities?

And so, the investigation on the Syndicate began.

The investigation has still been ongoing. Black cryptocoins were being used to fund their operations, the money discreetly delivered to their Indus headquarters. What no one could still find out was the source of this money. The investigators suspected that very advanced AI were involved, that were not only responsible for deleting the ledgers for the transactions, but were feeding intelligence to the Syndicate, particularly on the investigators themselves. As soon as investigators would have a lead, they would lose it in seconds, as if their own memories were being wiped out.

One thing was clear though. The Syndicate was powerful and had benefactors that were not only wealthy people, but highly placed citizens, who in a clandestine way were expressing their belief and faith in the future of a new human race. As soon as the investigation started, the Syndicate had to stop all its activities. There was a chance it was going to be shut down permanently.

As time passed, the news died down and there was little interest in what happened in a remote part of the world called the Makran. And so, even when rumours had been going around that the CHB Syndicate has resurfaced after its initial shutdown, no one paid much heed. They had moved on to the next more sensational news.

The journalists have not been able to confirm the rumours.

CHAPTER 31

A New Life

Jahan Jumander was busy packing up all the items she had amassed from her different adventures, ready for the big move.

"I'll miss you," Erol said as he sat on the bed looking out the window. "It won't be the same."

"Stop being so melodramatic. I'm not leaving town."

"But you are leaving the hostel," Erol said, "and I won't get to see you as much."

"Maybe you can come over to my house then."

"*Your* house?" Erol added. "I wonder what Dr. Salim has to say about that."

Jay laughed. Recent events in the archaeology world had led to some great discoveries, and new appointments including the appointment of Salim Sarmo as the Dean of the Department of Archaeology at the University of Indus Science. The return of Sarmo to Kolachi meant that the Excavation Club would be revived once more.

"Well, will you come visit or not?" Jay stared into Erol's eyes and could have sworn he was getting redder.

"Maybe." Erol replied, as he shuffled his feet uncomfortably. "If I can find a ride."

"Well, how about you and I share the Tezla? You take better care of her than I do anyways."

Erol grinned as he leaned forward. "I do, don't I?"

"And I think she seems to like you."

"How could she not?" Erol winked at Jay, then leaned over and kissed her lightly on her cheek before he left the room.

Jay's heart did a light flutter, as she watched him walk away, leaving her to her packing. She felt warm inside and realized this is what home and belonging felt like.

The End

Printed in Great Britain
by Amazon